SUNSET STRIP

A TOME OF BILL ADVENTURE

RICK GUALTIERI

Edited by Megan Harris at
www.mharriseditor.com

Cover by Mallory Rock at
www.rocksolidbookdesign.com

Published by Freewill Press

DEDICATION

For Thomas Delgado.

ACKNOWLEDGEMENTS

Special thanks to: Solace, Jonathan, Jenn, and James.
Without your help, I'd still be shooting people with
Dessert Eagles and serving them a big heaping helping of
desert after dinner.

FOREWORD

Greetings and salutations, dear reader! The story contained within these pages takes place between the events of *Holier Than Thou* and *Goddamned Freaky Monsters*, books 4 and 5 respectively of the Tome of Bill series.

If you're just joining us, I would humbly suggest you start with *Bill The Vampire*, the Tome of Bill part 1 - albeit you are more than free to ignore my blathering and choose your own fate. Far be it for me to dictate the course of your entertainment.

For veterans of the series, having survived the previous books with (hopefully) your sanity intact, I bid you a fond welcome back. The following tale represents a bit of a departure from the norm. It's told from the viewpoint of Sally, Bill's snarky sidekick in the supernatural realm, and is perhaps a bit darker in tone as a result. I hope, though, in the end you'll agree that it is a more than worthy addition to Bill's universe.

Regardless of any of the above, I had a hell of a good time writing this story and sincerely hope you enjoy it.

Rick G.

1

"Faith is overrated."

"But you said..."

"Who gives a flying fuck what I said? I was talking out of my ass. Nobody has any idea where the hell he is. There hasn't been a single sign of him and, quite frankly, I'm beginning to think that standing around hoping he'll come back is a fucking waste of time."

I didn't mean to snap...well, maybe I sort of did. When one is in charge of a coven of vampires, one can't afford oneself the luxury of playing the role of good cop. By our very nature we're predators, in many ways not too far off from a wolf pack. The problem with predators, though, is that they always have their noses out, sniffing for weakness. You show it and you might as well save someone else the trouble and slit your own damn throat.

Complicating matters further the fact that vampires tend to be backbiting sons of bitches. That's not necessarily in our nature *per se*, but it's been ingrained in many of us as just the way things are done.

That's one of the few pains in the ass about being immortal. There's no such thing as just waiting for the boss to retire so you can take their position naturally. If you want to get ahead in the supernatural world, you'd better be prepared to knock someone else off the ladder - all while making sure your own grip is solid.

I locked eyes with Starlight and refused to blink. After a few seconds, she averted her gaze. We'd been playing this game for over twenty years and both knew how it was going to end. At this point it was just a matter of ceremony, nothing personal. We both knew that, too.

She was a good egg amongst a carton of rotten ones, a rarity amongst bloodsuckers. I had always liked her; maybe not quite at the sisterly level, but she'd never been on my shit list. That was a good thing for her because the only way off of it was as a pile of dust.

Still, there were appearances to be maintained. I couldn't afford to let this place turn into the *Sisterhood of the Traveling Pants*. That would be an open invitation for a challenge, and while I wasn't particularly worried about our current roster, it would be one more pain in the ass that I didn't need right now.

"So you really want us to give up, Sally?" She flashed her big brown eyes at me like she was a goddamn puppy instead of a creature of the night.

"I'm not giving up, Star. I'm just being realistic.

We've searched half the Tri-State area and have found jack shit. If Bill is out there, he doesn't want to be found. At this point, I say we give him the benefit of the doubt and assume that he'll be back once he's good and ready."

"But what if he's hurt?"

I smirked. She hadn't seen my partner in crime during that final battle with Remington's men three months back. Once he'd lost his shit, I doubt a tank would've been able to hurt him. To think that once upon a time there had been multiple Freewills - the legendary warriors of the vampire race - roaming about. That must've been terrifying for normal vamps, much less the enemies that they were supposedly used against.

Still, Bill had never stayed that way for long, at least the few times I had been present. His normal appearance was considerably less intimidating, both in form and function. Hell, half the time I could barely keep the doofus from tripping over his own two feet, especially whenever he started getting all gooey about either his wannabe girlfriend or keeping his humanity.

I let out a small sigh. Maybe Starlight had a point. However, since there wasn't anything we could do about it, there was no use in worrying about maybes.

"Vampires don't get hurt. We either heal or we're dust." That much was mostly true, albeit there were exceptions to the rule - shiny exceptions I considered as my mind turned to the silver stake in my top drawer...a little souvenir from that fight. Such things could put a nasty hurt on a vampire and keep us that way if someone really wanted to.

I pushed that thought from my head. Bill had enemies, no doubt about that. Still, I sincerely doubted many of them would keep him alive for sheer amusement. Even if they did, they certainly wouldn't be shy about bragging. As the only one of his kind in existence, he would make a trophy worth displaying for all to see.

"Trust me, there's no way..."

You will drown, screaming in a sea of filth!

Starlight jumped at the psychic outburst coming from the gleaming white skull atop my desk. She still wasn't used to it. By this point, though, it was little more than an annoyance to me.

"Oh, shut up," I muttered.

"It's still doing it?"

"Yeah." I turned my eyes toward the object. I probably should've gotten rid of it the second it started acting freaky. It couldn't have been a good omen of things to come, but still - it was my favorite paperweight. Besides, I had earned the damn thing.

"Do you think it's ever going to stop?"

"Hard to say." I ran my hand over it. "It's quiet for a while, and then just when I think it's done for good, it starts right up again."

"Have you tried...talking to it?"

I raised an eyebrow at the question as if such a concept was beneath my contempt. She didn't need to know that I had, of course, tried talking to it.

A week after Starlight had returned from upstate New York with Harry Decker's skull, the outbursts had started. In life, the guy had been an absolute asshole. In death, apparently nothing had changed. I had little doubt that had something to do with his former status as a master wizard. It seemed that his decapitated cranium still possessed at least a little of his mojo. Unfortunately, communication appeared to be a one-way street, kind of like some sort of fucked up Speak and Spell. There was no acknowledgement from the skull that it was self-aware...just random outbursts of crazy.

We waited a few moments to see if it would continue its tirade, but it remained silent.

"I'll have Monkhbat do one more sweep down near Bill's parents' place in Jersey." I could barely believe what I was saying. Some days I could be such a softie. Oh, who was I kidding? I was just using Starlight as an excuse not to give up myself.

She immediately brightened, and I rolled my eyes. "Last one. I mean it."

"No problem, boss," she replied, a smile spreading across her lips.

"And don't tell anyone." I made sure my tone implied that it wasn't a request. We were close enough in age that it would've been pointless trying to compel her - the vampire equivalent of mind control - but that still didn't mean I wouldn't make an example out of her if push came to shove.

Three months prior, I had taken over as acting master of Village Coven. This wasn't really anything different than before. Despite Bill holding the official title, I already ran the show from behind the scenes - quite well, if I did say so myself.

The problem was that shortly before he disappeared, the majority of our coven had been wiped out courtesy of the wad of meat that used to own the skull on my desk. Aside from Bill and me, only four others had survived. Two of them weren't an issue. The third hadn't lasted long, a consequence of his own stupidity. The final survivor of that massacre, though, was in the process of testing my patience...greatly. I had little doubt she was undermining me with the new members that had since been recruited.

Firebird and I had been turned at about the same time. In fact, she was the only member of the coven, including permanently deceased members, who I'd known during the days when I could still enjoy a walk in the sun without ending up a pile of dirt.

I allowed a few brief memories of those times to flit through my mind, then locked them up again. Those hadn't been the best days of my life. Then there had been the betrayal by Uncle...

No. I didn't have time for that crap. Besides, all of that was behind me now. Sure, I still had to deal with *him* on occasion, but despite his rank, more and more of the game pieces seemed to be falling on my side of the board lately. A good chunk of that had to do with the out of shape nerd that fate had dropped onto my lap - the one who, as it turned out, had more prophecies written about him than Harlequin does banal romances.

I put my business face back on. That was more than enough time spent worrying about Bill. The coven had to be my top priority, especially during *work* hours. Being a coven master definitely has its perks. The downside, though, is if said master isn't considerably more powerful or clever than the other members, that position can easily become tenuous. I had that second part locked up, no problem, but it was that first that made me sleep with one eye open.

The coven was currently back to about three-quarters strength. Our *recruiting* efforts had proved fruitful. About half were mine with the rest being strays left over from the battle that had ended with Bill's disappearance. I wound up *adopting* them since we had plenty of openings, and I kind of felt bad. They had all been employees of the other companies that occupied this building and had been caught in the crossfire by accident.

Unfortunately, but not surprisingly, a few had turned out to be assholes.

Newly turned vampires weren't a threat to me, but I didn't need some arrogant dickheads, drunk on power, giving me shit. Especially since, rumor had it, another coven in the area was greatly interested in our apparent weakness. We'd given them one hell of a bloody nose in past months, dusting their leader Samuel in the process, so it wasn't particularly surprising that they'd held a bit of a grudge ever since.

Impeding matters further was my suspicion that Firebird was busy currying the favor of some of the new recruits, no doubt in a pathetic bid to challenge me. Our power was about equal, but she wasn't quite dumb enough to face me openly. The end result wouldn't be in her favor. Instead, I suspected she was doing what she'd been since even before we'd both joined Village Coven: spreading her legs like the whore she was. Goddamn, men could be stupid. One didn't need the power of compulsion to make them willing slaves.

Needless to say, I had a lot on my plate. I just had no idea how much more shit was about to be dumped on it.

2

———

"I'm doing my best!" Cynthia protested.

God, how I hated when they whined.

She'd been brought on board less than a month ago after approaching me on the subway platform to beg for change. Possessing a keen eye for these things, I could tell she hadn't been on the streets for long. She had a glimmer of intelligence in her eyes, didn't reek of drugs, and quite obviously wouldn't be missed. In short, a match made in heaven.

Well, maybe not quite heaven. I'd put her to work manning a desk for the suicide hotline which served as the main source of food for the coven - gotta love takeout. Unfortunately, though relatively bright, she obviously wasn't cut out for the life of a counselor. At least, not the type I wanted.

"You're spending twice as long on the line as the others."

"I know, but I feel bad..."

I leaned down until my face was an inch from hers. "You need to get over feeling *anything*. This is a pure numbers game. If they're serious, or just a fucking attention whore, they go on this list. If they can be saved, you give them one of these referrals and get them the fuck off the line."

"I know, it's just..."

I tuned out the rest. Vampire newbs typically came in two flavors: ravenous monsters hell-bent on spilling as much blood as possible, and whining pussies unwilling to let their past humanity go. I wasn't sure which was more annoying.

Before I could chew her out, though, my overly-sensitive vampire ears picked up the elevator dinging open at our floor. I tensed up and turned toward the door. Considering the events of the past several months, one couldn't blame me for adopting a bit of a paranoid streak.

Cynthia continued to make pathetic excuses, but I ignored her and waited to see who or what was approaching. The cleaning crew had already made their rounds for the evening. The only member of the coven I was expecting was Monkhbat, and not for a few hours yet. Anyone else...well, with a single compulsion, the others would grab the firearms stashed around the office and fill the doorway with enough silver-coated lead to down a herd of undead elephants.

Sure, it was technically against the rules for me to arm the coven. The NYPD, the higher-ups who knew the truth about us, anyway, wouldn't be pleased if they found out. But fuck them. If the prophecies were true, they were all on the cusp of becoming an endangered species anyway.

I listened. A single pair of feet made their way to our front door. The owner wore what sounded like sensible pumps - definitely not Monkhbat. I held up a hand to Cynthia and she immediately shut up. She might've been new, but she knew the drill. I made sure that all the new vamps understood that powerful did not mean invincible. Most of the recently dusted members of our merry little bunch had been arrogant fucks, which hadn't exactly helped them in the end. A little bit of humility could go a long way during these crazy days in which we lived.

I directed all my senses toward the main door. There came a knock just as a familiar scent reached my nostrils.

The tension left me. Even had I not recognized our visitor, supernatural enemies hell-bent on destruction typically didn't waste time knocking. Go figure. Common courtesy is a dead concept in the world of the unnatural.

Curiosity immediately replaced apprehension. Why would she be visiting here? It didn't make sense. We weren't enemies, but we weren't exactly all buddy-buddy either. There was also the fact that we currently had a resident for whom her presence would incite quite a bit of violence. I had told Monkhbat's true master that she was dead. Finding out otherwise could cause some issues.

She was aware of it too. I had let her know during the last time our paths had crossed, months ago when

I had called to check on - and maybe threaten with bodily harm - her dumbass boyfriend.

Intrigued as to what would cause her to run the risk, I walked to the door and opened it.

"Hey, Christy. What brings you here?"

3

"This one is mine!" snarled a voice from behind me. His name wasn't important, something boring like John, I think. He was turning out to be one of the troublemakers, a sexist asshole who stylized himself as some sort of type-A leader. He was one of the leftovers from Remington's massacre, probably a dickhead middle manager during his mortal life. Give a guy like that a little power and he thinks he's lord of all he surveys.

It also didn't help that I was fairly sure he was a member of the group that Firebird had won over by use of her not-so-unique talents.

Goddamn, sometimes I hate newbs.

"Back off," I said without turning toward him. "She's not from the hotline."

Part of me was almost tempted to hold my tongue. Christy was a witch, a pretty potent one from what I'd seen of her powers. Flash-frying dipshit back there would probably barely work up a sweat.

I waited for a moment. John-boy might decide to press his luck anyway. It would give me a good gauge as to how much of a reminder the others needed as to who was in charge.

No attack came, though. He gave one more growl before going back to his duties. Good. There might still be hope for him yet.

Christy had put on some weight since last I'd seen her, no doubt a result of having been knocked up by her halfwit boy toy, Tom. Otherwise, she looked surprisingly good. Motherhood worked well for some women. I just hoped the kid took after her. God knows there're enough dipshits in the world as it is.

"Sorry for that bit of rudeness," I said. "They're still being housetrained."

Christy gave a half smile in return. "It's okay. I imagine I'm not..."

"What the fuck is *that* doing here?"

I stifled a sigh. I had thought Firebird was out for the evening, perfecting her blowjob skills.

"She's here under truce," I replied, turning to face her. "Run along and play, *Betty*. I'm sure there's an alleyway somewhere you can be making a quick buck in." I should have paid her the same heed as the other vamp. The redheaded slut thought she was my equal, but she wasn't even in the same league. Fuck that. She wouldn't have been able to afford a goddamn ticket to my ballpark.

She narrowed her eyes, probably more so at my dismissive use of her real name than my comment. She played the part of the not-so-blonde bombshell, but I'd known her before that. Hell, her hair wasn't even naturally that color...more of a mousy brown.

"Truce?" She raised her voice to get the attention of the entire room. "Isn't she one of the witches who's been trying to murder our leader, the illustrious Freewill?"

I rolled my eyes. *Illustrious Freewill?* Someone must've subscribed to the Word of the Day. Her usage was laughable, though. She'd been badmouthing him behind his back since the day he took over from Jeff, our previous leader. Unfortunately, Bill tended not to notice such things - he was usually too busy staring at her tits. Legendary Freewill he might be, but that didn't make him immune to being a desperate male.

She stepped dangerously close to me. "Is your position so weak that you'd consort with the creatures who have been trying to kill our master?"

Behind me, I sensed Christy tense up. Though I wouldn't shed any tears at seeing Firebird turned into a roasted turkey, this was my problem. The bitch had stepped way out of line. "Back off, Firebird. This isn't your concern."

"A real leader would have killed this *thing* the second the door was opened - but not you. My, how far you've fallen, little *Lucinda*."

Did she just say...? Oh, this two-bit tramp was definitely gonna get it.

I turned my head toward Christy. She had one eyebrow raised questioningly. I smiled and gave her a single shake of my head.

In that moment, Firebird - emboldened by the

fact that I'd broken eye contact with her - stepped up to me. Some people are just so predictable.

I waited for her to speak.

"Maybe it's time we picked a new..."

Without bothering to turn around, I brought my hand up - claws elongating mid-swing. Firebird was a lover - an undiscerning one, at that - not a fighter. I turned back to her just as she shrieked and raised her hands to cover her ruined eyes.

"You fucking bitch!" she screamed. "I'm going to..."

I should've torn out her tongue, too. I hit her again before she could finish the sentence, which shut her up as she fell to the floor. Oh well, being overly merciful has always been one of my vices.

I inclined my head to the two vamps nearest me, my meaning clear. They grabbed Firebird and dragged her from my sight.

I would be well within my rights to have killed her. Hell, a coven master was more or less free to do as they pleased. I briefly remembered back to Jeff's reign. He was an asshole for whom there was no such thing as too much abuse of power.

Unfortunately, she'd done her damage. Most of the others hadn't met Bill, but I'd been sure to fill their heads with as much bullshit about him as I could shovel. Firebird spilling the beans about Christy being one of Harry Decker's crew wasn't ideal. I didn't have to answer to any of them, but things were tenuous enough as it was. It was probably best to discuss matters with Christy elsewhere

All will be dragged screaming into a sea of boiling death!

Shit! The fucking skull was starting up again. Definitely time to go.

"Oh my God! That sounded like Har..."

"Truce is over," I snarled, grabbing Christy by the arm and steering her toward the exit. "Your kind is not welcome here."

Before she could say anything further, I opened the door and pushed her through. Turning back, I caught sight of Starlight.

"I'm taking this trash out once and for all. You're in charge while I'm gone."

I didn't wait for her acknowledgement before I slammed the door behind us.

4

"You in the mood for a drink?" I whispered once the door was shut. "Because I sure as shit could use one."

"Not with the baby," she replied, confused.

"Coffee it is, then. Come on, you're buying." I led her toward the elevator. Considering my show back there, it wouldn't do for anyone to walk out and find us having a friendly chat in the hall.

Unlike her boyfriend, Christy wasn't a complete moron. She followed and kept her mouth shut rather than argue. The elevator opened at our floor and we stepped in. I'd feel better once we were out of the immediate area, away from where the others could hear, see, or smell us...oh shit!

I put my hand in the door just before it shut. Fuck! I had forgotten about Monkhbat. Though tentatively under my command, he was far older than me. There was no way he wouldn't notice Christy's scent when he returned. That wasn't good.

I had lied to his master about her fate. Her having survived was easily explainable - magic, duh! - but me failing to sic the entire coven on her could be an issue if he blabbed. Thus, this needed to look a bit more convincing.

"What's wrong?" Christy asked warily.

"How's your magic?"

"Fine...now, I guess. I mean, I've been self..."

"That's fascinating. Can you do me a quick favor?" She nodded. "Good. Blast the shit out of the door."

"Why?"

"Monkhbat."

"Who?"

"Gan's lackey, the one I told you about."

Christy's eyes briefly flashed with power at the mention of the little Mongolian bitch. Those two weren't destined to be on each other's BFF lists anytime soon. Heh, I knew there was a reason I liked the witch.

"Don't feel you need to hold back. If anyone is too close to the door, that's their own fucking fault for trying to eavesdrop."

The elevator shut before the smoke cleared. Sure, it would mean some cleanup for the coven, but a little collateral damage was preferable to having my many lies unravel...lies that would, no doubt, leave me on the business end of an execution.

At some point, my house of cards would come

tumbling down, but today wasn't that day.

"You clawed out that girl's eyes," Christy said, breaking the silence.

"They'll grow back. How have you been?"

"A little tired."

"Still puking?"

"It finally stopped, thank goodness."

"So have you heard from..." we asked in unison, just as the doors opened to the lobby. Neither of us needed to reply to know the joint answer was *no*.

Goddamnit!

Christy held her tongue until we reached our destination, a little café in SoHo that served killer espresso. It was busy enough that our conversation would be lost amongst the inane chatter of the other patrons.

The waitress took our order and I finally got down to business. "Not a social call, I take it?"

She shook her head. "I need your help."

"Bill-related?" A glimmer of hope weaseled its way into my voice. Damn that fucking nerd for making me care!

"No. I was kind of hoping maybe you'd heard something."

"Yeah, but it's amounted to Jack and shit. I know he hasn't returned home, to his job, or his parents' house."

"Do you think he's..."

"Well, yeah; we're vampires. Of course he's dead."

She chuckled. It broke some of the tension.

Maybe now we could get to the point of the matter. It wasn't particularly smart for us to be socializing in public. I had little interest in getting my ass handed to me, no matter how good the coffee might be.

"It's Tom..." she started. Immediately, my attention waned. "His sister, actually." The twit had a sister? Now it was even less interesting to me.

"I assume this gets better."

"She's run off."

"So what? Is she, like, six?"

"Seventeen."

"Okay, well this has been fun," I said, standing up. "We'll have to do this again when there's an actual world-ending..."

"Wait, you don't understand."

"Understand what? That she had a temper tantrum because her parents didn't buy her a car or something?"

"It's vampires."

That caught my attention slightly. Normally I could give a shit about such things. I mean, I'm usually the cause of people's disappearances, not the other way around. Two things stopped me, though. Bill wouldn't have hesitated for a second to help his friend, and he'd certainly give me shit when he got back if I refused to do the same. Listening to him whine in my ear for all of eternity did not bode well for my continued sanity. Secondly, though I wouldn't have admitted it under torture by the Draculas, his fucking gimp of a roommate had helped us out on more than one occasion. I probably owed him just enough to hear Christy out.

I checked my watch. Oh fuck it, five more minutes wouldn't kill me. I sat back down. "Vampires?"

"Yes."

"Any of mine?"

"No. They're not from around here."

"Okay, start talking, but be warned; I'm ordering an appetizer too."

The waitress brought our drinks while Christy explained. She wasn't sure if it was coincidence or if some vamps had figured out two plus two and were purposely targeting Tom's family because of his association with Bill. Either way, his little sister had acquired a new boyfriend in weeks' past. He'd been stirring up trouble at home, driving a wedge between the girl and her parents...a not entirely difficult thing to do with a teenaged girl.

Tom, still preoccupied with freaking out at the concept of becoming a dad, hadn't paid it much heed. Couldn't say I blamed him. The prospect of siring a new generation of dumbass of his caliber could be off-putting to anyone.

Christy had likewise been busy, trying to keep him from turning into more of a dumb fuck than he already was, as well as apparently attempting to build a new mage coven. Hopefully it turned out to be more successful than her last one.

"So how do vampires play into this?"

"I'm getting to that," she said in between sips of a

decaf cappuccino. Ugh, the very thought made me gag. Talk about a sin against mankind. "Two weeks ago, Tom and I went down to visit with his folks. His sister mostly kept to herself, but I happened to see her new boyfriend once when he picked her up. Something about him set off warning signals."

"Something familiar?"

"Sorta." She broke eye contact. Before Bill's doofy charisma had won her over, she'd been firmly in the *kill all vampires* camp. "I didn't trust myself, though. Things are better than they were when I first found out I was pregnant, but my powers have still been going a little haywire every now and then. I've been self-binding myself just in case. It tends to mute everything."

"Self-binding? If we're gonna start talking kinks here, then I'm gonna need something stronger. Don't get me wrong, I like being tied up as much as..."

"No! My powers. I've been using a ritual to keep them in check."

"Oh, well that's a bit less weird...sorta."

"Anyway, as I said, everything's been muffled for me. All I got was a little feeling, like the hairs on the back of my neck standing up. The thing is, it kept nagging at me. So when I got back home, I decided to undo the binding and cast a scrying spell."

"In other words, you spied on them?"

"More or less."

"We're back to kinky again."

She ignored me. "I didn't get much at first."

"I take it you kept at it for a while?" I asked, bemused.

"Well yeah, she's Tom's sister. I mean, Kara's probably going to be my sister-in-law."

"Really?"

"Well maybe...someday," she replied, blushing. It was cute in a deer-in-the-headlights sort of way. "Anyway, the guy must've been real careful because I didn't see anything that would have set me off."

"Until…"

"I was scrying again two nights ago and found Kara and her mother in the middle of a massive blowout. I really just caught bits and pieces, but it was mostly about his age."

"College boy?"

"He's definitely a bit older than her."

"She wouldn't be the first girl to fall for a guy a few years her senior."

"I know. I have no idea what she sees in him, though. From the glimpse afforded me, he's nothing special. If anything, she's out of his league."

"Stupid and teenage girl tend to go hand in hand."

Christy nodded knowingly. "Anyway, the boyfriend showed up and got into it, too. That's when I caught it. It was only for the briefest of seconds, and I thought maybe I was just seeing stuff considering all the craziness we've been through the past couple of months…"

"He snacked on the mom?"

"Nothing that obvious. But his eyes turned black for just a moment. Too fast for either of them to notice, but I did."

"So what did you do?"

"I jumped in my car and drove down there."

"Wait, why didn't you just teleport? I've seen you do it before."

"Like I said, I've been binding myself lately. It takes a while to fully shake off. I wasn't quite up to snuff to travel that way. I could've made it, but would have been too tired to do much else if trouble started."

"Okay, fine. I don't need the details. So you and Tom…"

"Just me. He can get a little over-protective about his sister and, well, if things got ugly, I didn't want him getting hurt."

"Or fucking things up?"

She stared me in the eye for a moment before averting her gaze again. "Maybe a little of that."

Hah! Good to see she wasn't completely blinded by love. "And?"

"And I was too late. His sister was already gone, run off with that…"

"Filthy beast of the night?" I arched an eyebrow.

"Sorry."

I put my cup down. "Did you ever consider that maybe he's legit? Vampires aren't all bloodsucking monsters. I mean, there's Bill and…" I racked my brain, trying to think of another good example. Oh fuck it. "…and Bill. But I'm sure there are others like him. I mean, for all you know, they might really have something."

"Don't you think I considered that?" Christy asked, her tone clear she felt slightly insulted. "I know that in many ways you're just as human as I am."

I was tempted to correct her in that I wouldn't fall for a dorkus like she had, but I stopped myself short. That wasn't entirely true. Still, that was the ancient past, another life. I pushed aside those thoughts, avoiding that particularly gruesome memory lane.

Even so, it bugged me a bit. There was something disturbingly familiar with Kara's story. I'm sure it's that way with a lot of girls who wind up seduced by our kind. Here in the city, we tend to forgo the lovey-dovey shit and just lure our victims into a dark alley. Of course, half the time they're already hopped up on one drug or another. But not every place was like here, was it? In other parts of the country, they tended to move a bit slower. It still seemed like a lot of work for a meal, though.

"So what about the situation convinced you otherwise?" I asked, genuinely curious.

"While I was down there, I did some asking around about this guy."

"Just asking?"

"I may have befuddled a few minds in the process."

"When you've got it, flaunt it." She smirked. Maybe we weren't so different after all.

"Something like that. Anyway, it wasn't too hard to find out that he was from out of town…way out of town."

"How far?"

"Vegas."

"Really?" My curiosity piqued again. "Been a while since I've been out there."

"But you know people, right?"

"Well, yeah." I rolled my eyes. Hell, I had an in with one of the Draculas, our ruling council. One didn't get much more in-the-know than that.

"Good, because that's why I'm here. I'm heading out there and I need information."

"You're flying to Las Vegas?" She nodded. "That might not be too smart. What if you…"

"I won't. That's why I want your help. If you can find out how many there are and how old the coven master is, that'll give me enough to at least not go in completely blind."

"Whoa there!" I put my hands up. "Even assuming I wanted to rat out a den of vamps to you, they're probably just passing through. It's a popular tourist spot, even with my kind. They could be…"

"They're not. In fact, I know where they are."

"Scrying again?"

"Partly. But I really didn't need to. I broke into the apartment where this guy had been staying and found a couple packs of these."

She pulled a book of matches from her handbag and tossed it on the table in front of me. I glanced down casually at it and my eyes widened in surprise.

No fucking way.

I blinked and looked again, hoping my eyes had been playing tricks. There was no mistake. The words were as plain as the fangs in my mouth: *Pandora's Box*.

My breath caught in my throat as the name sank in. Memories, long since repressed, surfaced. It was like someone had kicked in a locked door inside of my mind.

Why that place?

5

"*F*ear *not, Lucinda, my dear. This shall remain our little secret.*"

"*Thanks, Uncle Colin. Mom probably thinks I'm waiting tables. She'd die if she knew…*"

"*You have nothing to be ashamed of, I assure you. You're a young, independent woman making her own way in the world. You should be proud of yourself. Now why don't you join us? You look like you could use a drink.*"

"*Are you sure it's all right? I don't want to interrupt.*"

"*Nonsense. Of course we don't mind. Have a seat. Allow me to introduce you to my friend, Jeffrey Pemberton. We were just out celebrating his recent promotion…*"

"Sally? Are you okay? Yoo-hoo, anyone home?"

"Huh?" I replied stupidly, pulling myself out of the memory.

"You zoned out for a second there. Are you all right?"

"Yeah," I said, still a bit shaken. "It's just that I know that place." Goddamnit! Why the hell did I just say that? It's not like Christy was anything even close to a confidant. Hell, I barely knew the chick.

Fuck! I thought I was finally past all that. The day I finally gave Jeff the last sunburn of his life was a new start for me. Why was it having an effect on me now?

"You've been there?" Christy asked, grasping the obvious.

Screw it. I decided to cut to the chase. Playing games at this point was meaningless. "That place is bad news. It's a meat market, in more ways than one."

"That's what I was afraid of. Do you think..."

"I *think* Tom's sister is in deep shit. If this vamp is connected to Pandora's Box, then best case scenario is she's shaking her goods on a stage for some question-able clientele."

"Worst case?"

"You're looking at her."

There was silence between us for a moment. Comprehension finally dawned on her face. "Oh...OH!"

"Here's the deal. I'm in, but my help doesn't come cheap." And with that, I somehow committed to action before common sense could remind me just how much this was not my concern. The goings-on with the coven must've rattled my brain more than I thought.

Christy eyed me dubiously. "How much..."

"Not money," I said. If only she knew what the

coven's portfolio looked like. "If I help you, I get Tom. He gets turned and serves me for all eternity."

"What?!" she screeched, spewing coffee and attracting the attention of the nearby tables.

A bemused smirk was my reply.

"That wasn't funny!"

"Sure it was. You should have seen the look on your face." As if I'd use him for anything other than perhaps one-time target practice. He's one of the few humans I'd be terrified of putting the bite on. With my luck, his idiocy would be contagious and I'd spend the next century drooling on myself and playing with plastic dolls.

"So what do you really want?"

"Only one thing: silence. I'll help you, but you don't mention this or anything you learn to anyone *ever*."

She considered this for a moment. "Agreed. We could seal our pact with a blood oath, if you want."

Blood oath? That sounded interesting...perhaps for some other time, though. I've always considered myself an old-fashioned girl when it comes to deals anyway.

"No need. I'll take your word for it, with the caveat, of course, being that if I hear otherwise..." I didn't need to finish. Christy knew enough about me to know that I wasn't exactly afraid to get my hands dirty. With a baby coming, she wouldn't be going out of her way to make more enemies than she needed.

Besides, even if she did blab, it's not like I wouldn't lie my ass off about it anyway.

She nodded, then got down to business. "Tell me what you know about that place."

"I can do better than that."

"How?"

"Easy. I'm going with you."

6

Christy was smart enough not to ask about the hows or whys of my reply. Hell, she was probably just glad to not be going alone with her idiot boyfriend. Performing a half-assed rescue mission straight into the heart of a powerful coven wasn't a particularly bright idea for anyone, no matter how much magic they might have at their disposal. That she was over three months pregnant meant she probably wasn't at her peak.

Tom would probably be wearing that stupid amulet of his, but that would just allow him to live long enough to watch his limbs get wrenched off. Don't get me wrong - even with me by their side, there was still a good chance we'd get our asses handed to us, but at least I had the advantage of knowing it in advance.

There was also the little fact, something I didn't make her privy to, that I wasn't entirely considering this a rescue mission. Though I didn't consciously admit it, this went deeper than that. Pandora's Box was where it had all started for me. Thirty years of fucking misery as little more than a slave.

Sure, it hadn't been all bad. Not to mince words, but I enjoyed an awful fucking lot of it. No matter how much compulsion is shoved through your skull, there are times when being a vampire - a predator amongst sheep - is completely and utterly addicting.

The rush of a mouthful of blood is incredible. It's what we live on and thus nearly all of our senses are heightened, amplified toward the goal of finding and devouring as much as we can. Blood, by itself, is more than sustaining to my kind. Every single drop is like the best meal you've ever eaten.

That's not all, though. I was never much into heavy drugs, but I'd dabbled back in the day. Maybe it's the rush of chemicals the victim releases, but blood fresh from a still beating heart makes a drug high pale in comparison. It goes from being a feast to ambrosia itself - a nose full of the best Columbian blow doesn't even come close.

That's part of the reason so many vampires are such animals. It's an addiction, pure and simple. Those who can subsist off of the bottled stuff don't know what they're missing. At the same time, though, they're lucky. They can control themselves, live almost normal lives. Some days I envy that...some days.

See, the rush is only part of it. Being a vampire is a heady experience. Even the meekest of the turned find themselves a lion prowling the Serengeti. The power, the near invulnerability; it's every bit as addicting as a successful hunt. Imagine if tomorrow you woke up to find yourself completely above the law, with almost no consequences for your actions - at least in normal society. It's something like that.

We have rules, sure, and our own hierarchy. Step outside of that and you can find yourself back at the bottom of the food chain faster than you can blink. But even so, there're a whole lot more humans than there are vamps. Even the lowest of us is a lord when walking amongst them.

That's what most of us try and fool ourselves into believing, at least. The truth is a bit more complex. Vampire society is often times little better than a caste system. There are leaders, soldiers, and then there are the rest - those who are little more than shit upon the boot heels of the masters.

Most don't realize that. It's almost pathetic. The rabble of the undead often fool themselves into thinking they're gods amongst men when, in reality, they're little more than what they were in life - maybe even less.

You see, vampires tend to be very selective about who they turn. It's not what you think, though. The vampire nation isn't always on the lookout for the best and brightest - quite the contrary, in fact. True leaders are rare amongst the undead.

Don't believe me? That's fine, but I'm here to tell you if that were the case, every great person who ever lived would now be an immortal creature of the night.

I'm sorry to say, but that doesn't happen often. Sure, Alexander the Great walks amongst our kind, and we formerly counted Ogedai Khan, son of

Genghis, in our numbers, but that's more the exception than the rule. You won't find many others. No FDRs, JFKs, MLK Jrs, or Abe Lincolns wander the night seeking the flesh of the living. Hell, sad to say, but not even Elvis made the cut.

Most that are turned are easily controlled - cannon fodder for their betters. They exist as forces to keep us strong, but can be sacrificed without a second thought if the need arises.

Why? It's simple. Leaders want to lead, not follow. An entire society based on the best and brightest would erupt in civil war as countless factions each tried to seize control. We would go extinct fairly quickly, not from outside forces, but from within - staking each other in the back as we did so.

Thus, often times, it is the weak-minded but able-bodied who are brought into the fold.

The thing is…sometimes they make a mistake. Bill is definitely one such miscalculation, whether or not he wants to believe it.

Most don't realize I'm one, too.

I hung up the phone. Speaking with James almost always made me feel better. He was a rarity amongst the rare…a vampire with the brains to lead and the foresight to make sure what he was doing was for the greater benefit. You'd be hard pressed to find another vamp like him. Don't get me wrong, he wasn't a pushover by any means. Those who crossed him often didn't get a second chance. His allies, though, were treated quite well. Take me, for instance.

I'm fifty...well, something. Never ask a lady her true age, especially one that can snap most men's necks like a toothpick. Regardless, I'm but a babe in the woods compared to some vampires. James is one of the Draculas, the *First Coven* - our ruling council. Only the strongest and smartest get to play ball for that team. James wasn't the oldest vamp out there, but I had personally seen him edge out others who had greater experience on their side.

The thing is, the Draculas were well known for not tolerating what they called "children." Most vamps under a century in age that tried to seek an audience with them would be taught a lesson in respect that they...well, those around them, anyway...would never forget. That I had James's personal cell phone, as well as an open invitation to use it, was almost unheard of. Thankfully, I had a few plusses in my column. Being allied with the legendary Freewill certainly didn't hurt. James and I also had history together. A history of mutual, if not entirely equal, respect.

I had felt like shit as of late for lying to him about some of the things that had gone down here in New York. Still, mutual respect was one thing, but a death wish was quite another. Had I spilled my guts to him, it most likely would have resulted in more guts being spilled - mine chiefly.

Because of that guilt, I felt the need to tell him of my intent to visit Marlene's territory. If things went badly, which was an almost one-hundred percent likelihood, then at least he wouldn't be caught off guard.

Typically, spats between covens were considered a personal matter. The Draculas were our lawgivers, but they weren't our babysitters. We were expected to handle a lot of intra-vampire shit on our own. It wouldn't do to have a bunch of apex predators come crying to their mommies every time their feelings got hurt.

These days, though, things were different. We were on the eve of war. Bizarre happenings were going on all over the world as we and our allies prepared to do battle with our ancient foes. Because of this, I felt it was a good idea to give the heads-up in a case where there was potential to thin our ranks a bit. I hoped it didn't come to that, but...

Wait, did I really just think that?

Goddamnit, Bill's simpering humanity must've really been weaseling its way into my frontal lobe. I really needed to stop with that shit...maybe kill some old ladies or burn down an orphanage to get my mind back on track.

Of course, I wouldn't exactly mind if shit turned bad while in Vegas...at least, as long as it turned bad in my favor.

Marlene and Pandora's Box was where it all started for me. It was where I...

No, that wasn't quite right. In all fairness, it started long before then.

7

1969

"Lucinda Marie Carlsbad, do you have any idea how long our mother has been calling for you?"

My sister, Linda, stood in the doorway of the bathroom, hands on her hips. She considered herself an adult, far too sophisticated for her fifteen years of age. She often acted like she was forty years older than me instead of just four. Personally, I just considered her a stuck-up bitch.

"I heard her," I said as I lifted the hot appliance, lest it start to burn, and inspected myself in the mirror. "I'm not finished yet."

"What are you doing?"

"Ironing my hair."

"Why?"

"I saw a picture of it. Looked neat."

"On someone good-looking, maybe. It's going to look stupid on you."

"Not as stupid as your face," I spat back.

"At least I have a pretty one. Nobody's ever going to like a bookworm like you."

I lifted my eyes briefly in her direction. One word flashed through my mind: *cunt.* I stifled a giggle as the most forbidden of the forbidden words danced at the tip of my tongue. It fit her to a tee.

Tall like our father, she was slim with full-bodied hair. No matter what she said, I didn't think she was nearly as beautiful as some of the women in the fashion magazines that Mama liked to read. Even so, she had her pick of suitors at school, especially ever since she had graduated from a training bra. All the while, I could still pass for a boy with my shirt off - not that I'd ever even dream of taking mine off in front of one.

I decided to stifle the words begging to be released. Linda would probably just use them as an excuse to get me into trouble. "What does she want?"

"It's not a child's place to question her elders." I stood and stared at her, refusing to take the bait. Finally, she relented. "Dad's bringing someone home for dinner, an important investor at his firm. Mama wants us tidied up and downstairs."

My eyes opened wide. Our father mostly left the discipline to our mother, but his job was one place where we knew not to step out of line. If he was bringing some bigwig home, then he was expecting dinner to be on time, his wife to be beautiful, and his daughters to be respectful.

My dress had been slightly wrinkled the last time he'd brought a guest home and I'd caught three weeks of grounding for it afterward. Now, here I was with half my head ironed, the rest looking like a rat's nest of curls.

"What time?"

Linda leaned against the wall and smiled wickedly. I got a bad feeling in my gut.

"In about fifteen minutes," she said. "I told you, Mama's been calling."

I'd learned my lesson about the dress from the last time. Though I only wore them during times such as these, I made it a point to keep a few hung up neatly in my closet at all times. Maybe I'd never be as glamorous as Linda, but she wasn't even close to being an A student like me - with maybe the exception of the occasional B minus in math. Once was often enough for me to get the drift.

It was a simple matter to throw one on over my shirt and shorts. My hair was another matter entirely, though. There wasn't time to finish straightening it and Linda would have sooner swallowed a frog than help me out. A ponytail was out of the question. Daddy considered them unladylike. It would just get me grounded again.

Tears rose in my eyes as panic began to set in, but then I remembered the magazines. I quickly shoved aside the stack of history textbooks on my bed, locating the issue of Cosmopolitan I'd borrowed from Mama's bureau. It held a look that might just work...a tight bun on top with a few errant curls escaping. I began flipping through the pages. If I could pull it off, I might just survive the night.

Mama gave a sniff as I ran into the kitchen to grab the place settings. It rang of disapproval. I'd checked myself in the mirror against the photos maybe a dozen times in hopes of pulling off the look. Obviously, I hadn't. My sister's grin burned a hole through me. That was the worst of it. Though I'd miss my friends, I could handle being punished. Dealing with Linda's smug attitude was the real torture.

She was everything a perfect daughter should be: pretty, popular, interested in the things Dad thought she should be. She'd be sure to make some lucky fella a happy little baby factory one day. I, on the other hand, would have been better off being born a boy. If that had happened, I'd have probably gotten a pat on the back and a "Go get em, Tiger!" at every possible turn. As it was, my father constantly bemoaned me under his breath, wondering where I got my ideas from and lamenting me not knowing my proper *place*.

The sound of a car pulling into the driveway dragged me from my thoughts...foolish daydreams, as my father would say. The headlights of the family sedan momentarily flashed through the front windows. There was no time to fix my hair into something acceptable. As Mama ushered us all into the living room to greet Dad and his guest, it was clear that I was sunk.

"Honey, I'd like you to meet Mr. Kennelsbeth," my father said brightly. I forced a smile as he made his customary introductions. Unfortunately, I'd seen the brief shadow cross over his face as he walked in the door, performing a cursory once-over in my direction. "Mr. Kennelsbeth is a very important investor in my firm."

"*Potential* investor, Roger," the man chuckled. "Let's not get ahead of ourselves." He was tall and thin with neat black hair. I didn't know much about men's fashion, but even I could tell his suit must've cost a lot more than the brown slacks and sport coat my father wore. He had very alert eyes that seemed to take in everything and everyone at once. On a lesser man they might've been considered shifty, but I was sure Dad would insist that a man of Mr. Kennelsbeth's caliber should be considered shrewd instead.

He extended a hand to my mother. "Please, call me Colin." My eyes opened wide. I'd never seen such neat hands before, not even when Linda and Mom treated themselves to manicures.

"It's rude to stare, Lucinda." My father's tone was jovial, but his gaze icy.

"Nonsense," replied our guest as he turned toward us. He gave my sister a quick glance before focusing all of his attention on me. For just the barest of moments, a blush rose to my cheeks. "Lucinda, was it? A pretty name for an even prettier girl. Why, you look just like a Hollywood starlet."

My blush deepened. "Thank you, Mr..." I stammered.

"None of that," he corrected. "As I said, you may call me Colin."

"Thank you, Col..." I stopped as I caught my father's glare.

"Mind your elders, Lucinda. I'm sure *Mr. Kennelsbeth* was just teasing."

"Hardly," the man replied with a chuckle. "I flew in just last night from Los Angeles. Believe me, your little Lucinda here has fashion sense that would make the girls in Beverly Hills jealous." He looked thoughtful for a moment. "How about a compromise, Roger? I dare say, having met your charming family, I find myself warming to the idea of our partnership. How does Uncle Colin work?"

My father gave a nod and smiled, obviously far more pleased with the business prospect than whatever I would be calling our visitor.

"Excellent!" Uncle Colin beamed. "Now why don't we sit down to that meal you raved about earlier and you can tell me all about your plans to shrink those machines down. The thought that they might one day fit into something as small as a closet intrigues me greatly..."

8

I stood in front of the small private terminal in La Guardia. I'd weighed the pros and cons of making a quiet entrance into Vegas, but finally said fuck it. Flying commercial was about as much fun as being gang-staked. Though it might've been smarter to do so, this way had its advantages too. With Bill on the lam, I was officially on the books as the master of Village Coven. Being that my little group had gotten far more attention than usual as of late, there was a bit of status afforded me.

Chartering a private jet through official channels would send a message to Marlene that I was on equal standing with her. Though nobody on our end would be giving her a call to let her know I was incoming - least of all me - I was also well aware of how she ran things. As leader of the most powerful coven in the City of Sin, she made it a point to know when to expect company. It was her way of maintaining an edge. Ranking vamps would be shown the time of their long lives, no invitation necessary. Potential rivals would be kept a close eye on and dealt with accordingly.

She was smart. I needed to keep that in mind. She was also a lot older than me. On her home turf, nearly every advantage would be hers.

So we're fucked. What else is new? a small voice in the back of my head replied in Bill's voice. It was almost enough to make me crack a smile. While I fought down a grin, a car pulled up.

"Aren't we missing someone?" I asked as the cab's lone occupant disembarked with her bags.

"Tom's not coming," Christy said as she approached. Her eyes spied the dark, seemingly run-down building behind me. "We *are* flying, aren't we?"

Alas, one can't bullshit a bullshitter. Though not exactly sorry to hear that I wouldn't have to listen to him stupiding up the entire four-hour flight, I was curious nevertheless. "So does he hate his sister or something?" I could definitely relate to that concept, even if it did annoy me to have something in common with the meatsack.

"When are we leaving?" She tried to walk past me. Heh, good luck with that. Anyone trying to step foot uninvited into a vampire-owned facility like this would soon find themselves wishing for a TSA full body cavity search. As amusing as that might be to watch, I decided it was probably best saved for another time. Before she could sidestep me, I nimbly placed myself in front of her.

"Spill," I commanded, folding my arms across my chest.

She sighed. "He doesn't know."

"Doesn't know? Doesn't know what? That you're flying Vamp-air? That you invited me on this little expedition? That..."

"Any of it!" she snapped. "He doesn't even know that his sister is in trouble. As far as he's concerned, I'm just going on a business trip for our firm."

I raised a questioning eyebrow. "Really? Isn't he going to be a bit pissed? I mean, we're talking his sister, his pregnant girlfriend, and not to mention, several potentially unfriendly vamps."

"Mad is better than dead."

"I'll give you that. You mucked with his head again, didn't you?" My admiration of her raised a notch.

"There was no need. He's otherwise occupied."

"How so?"

"I put him to work setting up a baby registry. That'll keep him busy for days."

"Slick," I said. "Although choose carefully. I have to warn you, you're talking to someone who doesn't shop at any place below Nordstrom." She smiled a bit. Gah, I needed to watch it. I really was slipping. Used to be I'd gut someone as soon as look at them and here we were acting like this was fucking *Thelma and Louise*.

Before we started singing Kumbaya, I steered us back to business. "What about anyone else? I mean, aren't his parents going to..."

"They don't know either." She averted her eyes.

"How? Didn't you say..."

"I never said I didn't muck with *their* heads."

Damn! I couldn't help myself with that one. My cool demeanor collapsed into a chuckle. "Way to deal with the in-laws. I don't think that one ever happened on *Bewitched*."

"It was necessary."

"You don't need to justify these things with me. Aren't they going to notice her gone, though?"

"Nope. They'll think they see her out of the corner of their eyes and will remember talking to her...after the fact, of course."

"Pretty slick."

"Thanks. Mind magic has always been one of my specialties. Harry used to say I had a real knack for it."

"Harry used to call me a diseased trollop."

There was a momentary awkward silence. "I guess we saw different sides of him."

Stone-faced, I turned toward the entrance of the terminal. I'd seen a different side of him, all right. Hell, I had a part of his *inside* sitting on my desk back in Manhattan...not that she needed to know that.

"I'm surprised you haven't asked about him," she said to my back.

"Decker?"

"No, Ed."

My hand paused on the door handle. "How is he?" I asked nonchalantly.

"Good. Settling into his new role nicely."

I didn't ask anything further. She, likewise, didn't need to know that I was well aware of that. I'd kept Bill's apartment under surveillance ever since he'd disappeared. It was entirely for the purpose of keeping an eye out for his return...

...or so I kept telling myself.

"Care for a drink?"

"Red wine, please."

I cocked an eyebrow. I'd have figured Christy for the no smoking, no drinking type while pregnant.

"One won't hurt," she said. "And I sorta don't like flying."

I burst out laughing next to the wet bar of the private Boeing 737.

"Why do you think I use my magic so much?" she asked, buckling herself securely into one of the leather seats.

"Guess that means not much flying on broomsticks." I found a nice Merlot for her, then opted for something a little stronger for myself. Ooh, make that stronger *and* more expensive. I picked up a bottle of thirty-year-old Cognac. Yes, that would do nicely. It's good to be a coven master - one who understands the concept of pulling strings. Poor, Bill. One of these days, he was gonna figure out...

I let the thought drop. Worrying about where he was and in what condition wouldn't do me any good right at that moment. Regardless of the style in which we were flying, we were still heading into a lion's den. Distractions were never a good thing when dealing with the vampire nation. Fortunately, Christy was there to pull my focus back on track.

"What can you tell me about Pandora's Box?" She closed the blind to the window closest to her, despite it being pitch black out. Damn, she really was skittish about flying.

I handed her the wine glass and sat down opposite her, feeling the slight tilt of the cabin as we continued to climb toward cruising altitude.

We had about four hours to kill. That was more than enough time to fill her in on Marlene and the Pandora Coven, as they were unoriginally named. The only questions in my mind were where to start and how much to tell her.

"Take off your top."

"Now?"

"Yes, now. And before you ask, yes, right here. This is the gig, so you'd best get comfortable with it."

"Oh...okay."

"You're going to have to get over it if you want to survive here, girl. If not, go back home to the farm or wherever you came from. Either way, it's no skin off my teeth...There, see how easy it was? Move your hands out of the way. That's better. See, not so hard, is it? Very nice, very nice indeed. Oh, relax already; they're just breasts. I'm going to let you in on a secret. They're both your greatest asset and best weapon here. Don't be shy about using them. Now, let's see the rest..."

The choice was clear, but I didn't like it. Hell, I'd have put my fist through the wall to vent some frustration if a little thing called explosive decompression wasn't a concern.

Some days I envied Starlight and Firebird. Though they had radically different demeanors, they had one thing in common - an overabundance of heavy thoughts didn't weigh down either of them. There were times when I thought that would be a minor blessing. Sure, I'd be destined to forever remain someone's minion, but others could handle the heavy lifting and I could just keep the party going until such time as our enemies overran us.

Alas, I'm not so lucky.

Christy and I were on good terms for the time being - a minor miracle, considering that her former coven almost completely wiped out mine recently. Still, she didn't have anything to do with it, and I was willing to overlook that matter. Even so, I didn't see us ever going out for pedicures together. At the end of the day, we ran in different circles. Also, she was fucking someone I considered to be a base idiot at best.

The problem was, despite being knocked up by a moron, she wasn't one herself. I had little doubt she'd notice if I held back on anything important. There was also the possibility that doing so might inadvertently screw us over during a critical juncture in this endeavor. I let out a heavy sigh. There really wasn't much choice.

"What I'm about to say stays between us."

"Sure..."

"No, you don't understand. I mean it. You don't tell Tom, you don't tell Ed, you don't tell your baby one night as a bedtime story, and you especially don't tell Bill. This is pain of death stuff. I don't need to remind you that when vampires decide you're going to hurt...you're going to hurt."

She glared, obviously not appreciating the threat. I could respect that, but I sure as shit wasn't afraid of her. On a good day, any throwdown between us would probably have an even chance of going either way and she knew it. Right now, the advantage was mine. She wasn't in peak physical condition and she needed my help.

Christy finally nodded. "Does everything with your kind have to end in a death threat?"

I shrugged nonchalantly. "It's what we do."

"Very well. If it will help, then I swear by the White Mother what is said here is between us and us alone."

I had no fucking idea who the White Mother was, but I broke the tension with a smile anyway. "What happens on the way to Vegas, stays on the way to Vegas."

"That doesn't make any sense."

"Who cares? You want to hear this story or not?"

9

"I worked for the vamp that runs Pandora's Box. Her name is Marlene."

"So she used to be in New York?"

"No."

"Did you...somehow transfer covens?"

"Not quite. I worked for her back when I was still human."

"Oh!" Her eyes opened wide in surprise. "I never knew. I just sort of assumed..."

"I was an East Coast girl? Yeah, I could see how you'd get that idea. What can I say? New York living has been kind to me."

"So...what did you do for her?"

I stood to walk back to the bar as the jet passed through some slight turbulence. Grabbing the Cognac, I refilled my glass, but decided to bring both back with me to my seat. The memory I was dredging up required a three-drink minimum.

"I did what I imagine Tom's sister..."

"Kara."

"Fine, Kara, whatever. Anyway, I did what I imagine she's doing right now."

Christy waited for me to continue. I'll admit, the pause was purposeful. I can't help but have an overdeveloped sense of drama.

"Pandora's Box is a strip club, although you probably already figured that part out."

She shrugged uncomfortably.

"You are familiar with strip clubs, right?"

"Not really. I mean, I've never been in one. The concept is kinda...gross."

I raised an eyebrow. "Hold on a second. Aren't your people the ones who popularized dancing bare-assed under the moonlight?"

"We call it communing skyclad."

"A rose by any other name..."

"It's different. It's a spiritual experience, opening ourselves to the magic around us. We allow the power that flows through the Earth to cover our bodies."

"Uh huh, and I'm sure the cops would still call it public nudity."

"Maybe," she snapped. "But at least we aren't letting men touch us for money."

"I think you have your Vegas professions mixed up."

"Are you telling me none of that goes on at this Pandora's Box?"

She had me there. Marlene and her staff would often turn a blind eye to such things for those who cared to make a little money on the side.

"How can you just...do that, Betty?"

"How? It's pretty easy how. It's the difference between going home with five hundred in my pocket and two thousand."

"But how can you just let them..."

"Are you really that naïve, Lu? Don't tell me you've never just lain there and taken it with that boyfriend of yours. I'm doing the same thing, with the exception that they pay me to leave afterwards."

"If she's just dancing, then she's probably okay. That's the least of what goes on there. The problems begin when you start to slip further down the rabbit hole."

"Vampires?"

"Eventually. Especially if she catches one's eye."

"Her boyfriend..."

"We don't know shit about him. He could just be a lackey or he might be a player like..."

"Like?"

"Like Jeff."

"Who's Jeff?"

"Nobody anymore. Let's not worry about him at the moment. Bottom line is, we don't know what we don't know."

The silence grew between us for several seconds.

"So, how'd you end up there?"

"That one is easy. It was the late seventies. The world was flip-flopping between being one big party and completely losing its shit. Carter was busy screwing up the economy. It was a good time to be aimless."

"Bad family life?"

"Nothing like some of the horror stories you hear. But it wasn't great. My dad pretty much browbeat any sense of ambition out of me by then. In his eyes, a woman shouldn't look forward to anything more than finding a good man to settle down with and get knocked up by. Reading, writing, and arithmetic were just distractions to keep us out of trouble until Mr. Right came along. I might've managed to escape that, but my mother was a jellyfish. Then there was Linda. She was more than happy to play the ideal woman for dear old Dad. She was all about cheerleading, helping with supper, and thinking no further ahead than the edge of her bra."

"Linda?"

"My bitch of a sister. What a pair we were - Linda and her bookworm of a baby sister, Lucinda. God, what the fuck were my parents thinking with those names?"

"Bookworm? Wait, your name is Lu..."

I glared at her. "My *name* is Sally. That other girl died a long time ago." I leaned forward and looked her in the eye. "This is one of those pain-of-death moments, in case you were wondering."

Christy held her hands up in a placating manner.

"Anyway, I had given up on bettering myself, having long since swallowed dear old Dad's Kool Aid. However, I still had enough teenaged rebellion in me to want to get the hell out."

"Where were you headed?"

"Nowhere...everywhere. Maybe I had some grandiose plan of hitchhiking across America. I don't know. Made it about fifty miles before my babysitting money ran out. Care to guess where I ended up?"

"A place with a knack for gaudy casinos?"

I touched the tip of my finger to my nose. "Got a job waiting tables at an all-night café and managed to get a room in a flop house at the very edge of the city. Lot of hard luck cases there, but they mostly left me to myself. I met someone...a guy named Mark who bussed tables over at the Hacienda with eyes toward running the roulette wheel one day. He wasn't anything special to look at, but he treated me well. I'm sure it wasn't much different than a thousand other stories there."

"So then you decided to get a job dancing at Pandora's Box?"

"No. I never even thought about it. Would never have pictured myself at a place like that because I'd have never thought they'd hire someone like me."

Christy's face took on a dubious expression as she eyed me. I could understand the confusion. Not to toot my own horn, but I am well aware of my assets...at least, these days I am.

"My sister was tall, about five-seven," I explained. "She was pretty stacked, too. Definitely was never hard-up for a date come Friday night." I stood up to emphasize my point. "Me, I took after my mother. She was a petite thing. Would've had trouble topping five feet in stilettos...not that Mom would've been caught dead wearing them. No, wasn't her style. She was more the Marion Cunningham type. Anyway, my sister made it a point to remind me about my short-comings at every opportunity."

"Why did you listen to her?"

"You try listening to the same crap for years on end and tell me if it doesn't have a way of weaseling its way into your skull. Do I need to remind you how evil you were convinced the Freewill was?"

"Point taken." She averted her eyes. It was a bit of a low blow on my part, but I could see she immediately understood my point.

"Anyway, you get my drift. As I grew, my tomboy looks went away. I mean, I never quite got a growth spurt, but I definitely filled out in other areas. The problem was, in my head, Linda's voice kept telling me over and over what an ugly fucking duckling I was. As far as I was concerned, I was a frump. I played the part, too. Heh, thinking back on it, Mark was a bit of one too, although in his case it was real. He probably couldn't believe his luck that he had all *this* on his arm come his night off."

"So where does Marlene play into this?"

"I'm getting to that, relax. Anyway, my normal way of dressing was nothing to write home about. God, if I could go back in time, I'd probably beat myself to death with a copy of *Vogue*. The place where I worked, though, eventually got bought out by a new owner. The guy decided to try sexing up the joint. He made us wear uniforms...tight ones, not entirely unlike what you might see at Hooters. Personally, I was mortified to dress like that, but a job was a job.

There weren't many other choices, so I did what I had to do."

I paused to take an extra-long sip of my drink. From this point forward, we'd be tripping over the skeletons in my closet. "And that's when it happened. One night, this slick dressed guy comes in for a cup of coffee. He was eyeing me up the entire time he was there, making me wonder what the hell was wrong with me. I practically died in my skin, thinking that he was disgusted at what he saw - a mess like me in an outfit like that."

"But you were wrong."

"Exactly. Before he left, he pulled me aside. Said a girl like me could be making a hundred times what I was earning at that dump, then handed me his card. Can you guess what was written on it?"

Christy smiled in response, although it didn't reach her eyes.

It was a sentiment I could very much understand.

10

————

We touched down a little over two hours later, taking the time zone differences into account. That left plenty of the night ahead for us, or at least for me. Christy was looking a bit green about the gills by the time we stepped off the jet. Go figure. Some people just have no constitution.

I guess I couldn't blame her much. Three quarters of the way into the trip, red lightning began to flash around us, a definite unnatural occurrence. More and more such freak storms had been happening across the world as of late. It was a sign of the impending battleground that the Earth was about to become. More often than not, strange sightings or disappearances followed. A small part of me briefly wondered what the headlines would read once the sun came up.

There wasn't time for any of that, though. We had business to attend to. Unless creatures from beyond the veil suddenly overran Vegas, we had to keep our wits about us.

Following the storm, I'd given Christy a chance to regain her equilibrium, even being so nice as to not make fun of her for it...much, anyway. I then instructed her to change her clothes. It wasn't that she was covered in puke or anything gross like that, mind you. She wasn't showing much yet, but the slight bulge in her midsection could potentially give her away on the ground. Vampires are masters at spotting and exploiting weakness. Marlene, being head of an enviable coven in a city known for its nightlife, had developed this to a near art form. An obviously pregnant foe might as well just save everyone the trouble and gut herself.

Fortunately, possibly for both of us, Christy still had some fight in her. Though a little wobbly from our aerial acrobatics, she put her hands up, muttered a few words, and a flash of light later, you'd have thought she was ready for bikini season. Her clothes were now practically falling off of her.

"It's a glamour," she explained. "A pretty advanced one, hard to spot or sniff out. My people developed them during the Inquisition, albeit they used it for different purposes back then. Was the only way we kept from being wiped out."

"How long will it last?"

She cocked her head in response. "Hopefully long enough."

Gotta love confidence.

"So do we head straight over to..."

"No," I stated flatly. "Follow me. A car's waiting."

"Where..."

"To the MGM Grand. I booked us a pair of adjoining suites. We're going to check in, relax for a while, then doll ourselves up and head downstairs to blow a few thousand dollars. Don't worry about your bags. The zombies will get them. That's what they're here for." I started walking, holding myself up as if I owned the place. Christy didn't need to know that I wasn't feeling much better than she was - just for different reasons.

"There are some very important clients flying in tonight. I want you to show them a good time, Lucinda."

"I'm not sure I understand what you mean."

"It's a private party, one of the rooms upstairs. You're to give them whatever they want, no questions asked. Don't worry, you won't be harmed."

"Won't be harmed?"

"They may get a little rough..."

"What? No. I don't do those kinds of things. Talk to..."

"This isn't a request."

"Screw that. I'm not your whore. Ow! Let go of me!"

"You are whatever I say you are, girl. The moment you stepped foot into my club, you were mine. Don't fool yourself into thinking otherwise."

"You're crazy! I won't..."

YES YOU WILL!! YOU WILL DO AS TOLD AND TOMORROW YOU WILL FORGET ALL ABOUT IT!! YOU'RE HAPPY HERE, THAT'S ALL YOU NEED TO KNOW!!"

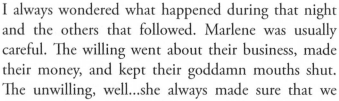

I always wondered what happened during that night and the others that followed. Marlene was usually careful. The willing went about their business, made their money, and kept their goddamn mouths shut. The unwilling, well...she always made sure that we never remembered a thing about what we'd done or had done to us. All we'd know is that we'd wake up the next morning with cash in our purse and an oddly upbeat attitude about what we did for a living.

There was just one small problem: she'd been sloppy with that first compulsion. I still had no idea what happened afterward, but she hadn't erased the act of compulsion itself from my mind. Thankfully, nothing escaped my lips to the contrary at the time, although I'd be lying if I said it wasn't out of fear. For a time, I had no idea what it all meant, other than perhaps I was going crazy.

It may have continued that way, possibly until I was too used up to be of any use to her. At that point, I'd have been casually tossed to the side like refuse if luck went my way. If it didn't...

My knuckles had turned white as my nails dug into the armrest of the limo. Pity - the rich Italian leather was no match for vampire claws. It was a shame to ruin something so beautiful, but knowing my kind, it hadn't been the first act of violence visited upon this vehicle.

The damage to the limo wasn't lost upon Christy, although she thankfully kept her mouth shut. On the walk over to where our ride awaited, I had mentioned that we were being watched. The air in the terminal reeked of the undead. Not surprising, considering we owned it. What was different, though, were the underlying scents. The smell of expensive cologne lingered at the periphery, stuff that the everyday staff probably wouldn't wear. Even with their enhanced senses, most vamps probably wouldn't have noticed it. Having been exposed to the finer points of city living, I had developed a refined nose for such things. It was easy for me to tell the difference between a spritz of Clive Christian Number One and whatever bargain fragrance was currently being hawked at Target.

It had been Jeff's one saving grace. He was an egomaniacal moron who demanded the very best and insisted his minions follow suit. If one cared to survive under his reign, one played the part. Tomboys became fashion models, country bumpkins became paragons of style, and so on.

The scents that lingered in the air were expensive ones. Marlene's people were close by. She had been there for years, worming her way into the nooks and crannies like a cancer, but no matter how hard she tried, even she couldn't be everywhere.

"Thank goodness for the mob," I muttered to myself.

"Eh?" Christy asked.

"Nothing," I replied, well aware that our ride was in all likelihood bugged.

We checked into our rooms at the Grand - adjoining suites on the twentieth floor. Executive level - nice, but not the top of the line. No need to look overly garish. Christy wanted to get some rest, and I couldn't blame her. I tried as well, but wound up pacing like a caged tiger, watching through a slit in the blinds as the sun arose over the city below.

It was going to be a nice day...for the living.

Hours later, as the sun started its descent, I changed into a dark red, off-the-shoulder mini dress. It was nice and befitting for the night ahead, which was a pity. While there was an off chance that things could be settled peacefully, I was prepared to see it go the other way.

Oh, let's face facts, I was betting on it. If that happened, I could probably count on my outfit being left in less than mint condition. Oh well. 'Tis the price we pay.

I applied makeup as usual, sending a silent thank you to fate that the silly pop culture belief of vampires casting no reflection was little more than bullshit. Then, I put on a pair of ruby earrings. Fortunately, any nastiness that ensued over the next several hours could probably be rinsed off of those. I kind of liked them.

A gold necklace with a heart charm rounded out the look and toned down the aggressiveness of my appearance a bit. Sometimes, the subtle things make all the difference between predator and prey.

When I was done, I knocked on the door connecting my and Christy's room.

It was time to kill a few hours.

11

Well, it would be time to kill a few hours *after* I fixed Christy up. She was still rocking her glamorized body. I had to admit, it beat the shit out of a CrossFit workout for instantaneous gratification. Unfortunately, the good news ended there. She was wearing slacks, a dull blouse, and a sensible sweater.

I couldn't help but roll my eyes. "You are not going downstairs like that. At least not with me."

"Do I need to remind you..."

"I know why we're here. I also know how we're going to get in there in the way that's the least likely to end with both of us taking a one way trip to the great beyond."

"Every second we waste is another that Kara could be..."

"What? Dancing on a pole? Getting dollars stuffed down her g-string?"

"Being turned," she hissed. Her eyes momentarily flashed with power.

"Not Marlene's style. Your wannabe sis-in-law doesn't have the right equipment to qualify for a promotion. Besides, I doubt anyone related to your boy toy is gonna show promise that quickly. True, Marlene used to occasionally make gifts of her girls to other covens...trust me on that one." My fangs momentarily descended as I fought to keep my emotions in check. "But that's not going to happen."

"How do you..."

"I talked to the higher-ups before we left. The vampire tourism trade is pretty dead right now. Between the oncoming war and the whole ordeal with the Icon a few months back, most covens are hunkering down...waiting to see what's coming. In short, they're scared shitless. Now stop trying to change the subject."

"I'm not going to..."

"As far as anyone who's seen us will assume, you're here with me. That means there are certain standards to be upheld. What you're wearing...it's embarrassing. Strip."

She stood there for a moment, a deer-in-the-headlights look on her face.

"I could always tear those clothes off you. I mean, some people are into that."

Her eyes opened wide in horror. My God, for someone who cavorted naked under the full moon, she sure was a fucking prude.

"You can wear something of mine if you want, but since you're about four inches taller, that's really gonna put the mini in miniskirt - which might work in our favor..."

As I turned toward the serious business of making Christy presentable, I sensed her frustration. Hell, the smell of it practically wafted off of her in waves. She probably thought I wasn't giving our mission the priority it deserved.

That's one problem with power - it doesn't instill in most people a sense of patience. The two combined can often end badly. That's one of the more hilarious secrets of the supernatural world. Vampires love to talk about living for all eternity, but it's been my experience that the majority of them don't make it past their first decade. If anything, many die well before they'd have done so naturally. It's that rush of power that does many in. They don't realize there's a vast difference between feeling invincible and actually being so.

Christy should have known better. By all accounts, she was a seasoned witch. Hell, her old coven had plotted meticulously to off Bill when they could have just come in at any time, guns a-blazing.

I couldn't bring myself to blame her, though. The last few months had been rough on all of us. Between the excess hormones pumping through her brain and being blinded by love, she was off her game. Add to that the death of her mentor, and she obviously wasn't firing on her usual number of cylinders.

Back when we'd first met, she and her asshole

leader, Decker, had blindsided us for a summary execution. I hated to admit it, but had their little party not been crashed by some vampire assassins - also out to snuff us, oddly enough - they might well have succeeded.

Now, though, her just wanting to charge into Pandora's Box, well...well, actually it was the sort of idiotic plan I'd expect Bill to come up with.

Dammit! There I go getting sentimental again. It really will be the death of me.

Christy cleaned up pretty nicely, if I do say so myself. How many other expectant mothers at the end of their first trimester could pull off the party girl look? Not many, I'd bet.

"I'm really not comfortable with this," she protested.

"Neither am I. Those shoes don't match, but it's the best we can do. Here, take this." I handed her a slip of paper.

"What is it?"

"A cashier's check for five thousand dollars."

"What for?"

"Sexual services, of course."

"What?!"

"Relax, Glinda. It's just spending money. We're gonna drop a small bundle at the tables, just like good little tourists."

"I'm not exactly an expert at gambling."

"Then you should be a natural at losing. When in doubt, go with what works."

Christy and I stopped dead in our tracks the moment we entered the casino, and it had nothing to do with the spectacle that is Vegas.

"You sense it, too?" she asked.

"No, but I sure as hell smell it."

I would've expected a variety of human scents to hit my nose, some more pleasant than others. I likewise wouldn't have been surprised to find a few vampires amongst the crowd.

What I didn't expect was the strange odor that hit my nose. Whatever the fuck it was, it wasn't human. The closest my memory could come to placing it was a vague similarity to the otherworldly beings from up in the northern tip of Canada some months back. A peace conference had taken place there, one that would've caused the eyes of even the most seasoned UN negotiator to fall right out of their head. A near endless array of beings had gathered to witness what turned out to be a botched effort to avert a war.

But it wasn't the same...whatever was here hadn't been one of the parties present up north. The scent was pungent, but not too intense. It was definitely not my imagination, though. There were other creatures here, blended in amongst the mostly human crowd. The only question was, whose side were they on?

Christy's arms instinctively went up in a defensive

gesture, but I grabbed her before she could do anything and shook my head. Whatever the fuck was going on here, we did not want to make ourselves a part of it.

"What is this?" she asked.

I steadied my voice. "If I had to guess, I'd say this city was on the verge of being royally fucked."

"Why here?"

At a temporary loss for words, I gave the best answer possible.

"Why not?"

12

_____

I am nothing if not resourceful. As the shock of the unanticipated non-human company wore off, my gears began spinning again.

Marlene had been in the game for about two-hundred and fifty years, having started out as a French courtesan. She'd never strayed far from her roots, but her power and influence on the West Coast were not to be denied. She'd established the Pandora Coven back in the nineteen-thirties and had kept it running strong ever since.

Even with my connections to the Draculas, I was going to have to do some fast talking if anything happened to her by my hand. I was fairly sure I'd be able to keep my ass out of the fire, but would almost certainly gain some enemies in the process.

But now...

Good, bad, or just plain bored, if there were beings from beyond the void gathering in this city, it meant just one thing: chaos. Accidents were bound to happen in such a state. I could work with that.

"Change in plans," I said to Christy out of the corner of my mouth.

"You never told me the original plan."

"Then it should be a piece of cake to modify."

"Okay, so we're out of here?"

"Fuck no. That part stays the same. Mama wants to drop some dimes at the tables. There's just a few parts of the new plan you need to be aware of."

"What?"

"Well, for starters, if I head back to the hotel, don't follow. Trust me on this."

There is one universal truth beyond the mainstays of death and taxes: a pretty girl throwing down hard cash at the craps table will never, ever have to buy her own drinks. It was the ideal place to be. A few wiggles of my hips, followed by the occasional girlish giggle when I won, and I was guaranteed to get some notice.

My original plan had been to allow Marlene to approach us first. Knowing our history, she'd have been suspicious had we headed to her place straight off. For most vamps, feeling suspicious equals putting up their guard. These days, that was bound to translate into stake first, ask questions later.

I had figured that if we minded our own business, eventually curiosity would overcome her caution and she would send in her people under the guise of hospitality. I'd seen her do it before, especially when the visiting vampires in question included a coven master.

"How'd you find this place, Uncle Colin?"

"Oh, I know the owner from way back."

"Marlene?"

"Is that what she's going by these days? Oh well, it doesn't really matter. Don't you worry your sweet head about it. Have another drink. This is a celebration, after all."

"I should probably go. Marlene doesn't like us to stay with one customer too long when it's this busy."

"Fret not. I'll have a word with her. You stay here and get to know Jeffrey a little better. I think he likes you."

The young man had caught my eye several minutes earlier, but I continued to ignore him. It was your typical game of cat and mouse, only I'm sure he thought he was playing the part of the cat.

From the way he moved, he was definitely human. That was good. As I was walking through the casino earlier, one of the beings present had turned and looked at me knowingly, obviously aware of what I was. On the outside, he looked human, but I caught a glimpse of jagged fangs, black as obsidian, when he threw a quick smile toward me. At this stage in my life, I didn't think teeth would unnerve me. I was wrong. I didn't know what the creatures mingling in this place were, but the chill up my spine warned me not to indulge my curiosity.

The clean cut man who was now walking in my direction, apparently having made up his mind that this game had gone on for long enough, wasn't some sort of ancient horror, but the way he moved told me he'd played this game before. Well built, good looking, and with sandy blonde hair, he reminded me a bit of Jeff.

That might have been enough to seal his fate then and there. The memories of this place begged for violent release. The arrogant swagger he put into his walk as he carried two drinks over, one obviously for me, said volumes toward the fact that unless he was supremely lucky he wouldn't be seeing the sun rise again.

Speaking of lucky…

"Seven!" the dealer called out. "The lady wins again."

I had to admit winning was far preferable to losing. When this was all over, I might have to splurge a bit with my not-so-ill-gotten gains. Perhaps a new snakeskin jacket. Maybe a...

"You've got the touch," my not-so-secret admirer said as he stepped up to the table.

"Not really," I replied, feigning an innocence I hadn't known in years. "I'm just throwing the dice. Guess they like me."

"They're not the only one."

Slick. Yeah, definitely a player.

I reached down to collect my winnings, then

stood and wiped a hand across my brow. "Woo, I'm feeling the pressure now."

"Well here then," he said, handing me a drink as if he just noticed it in his hand. "A little something to take the edge off."

"I don't know. I'm kind of a lightweight," I giggled, accepting the glass and taking a tentative sip. Ooh, a Mai Tai...tasty.

"I'm Tad."

"Lucinda," I replied, the name spilling from my lips before I even realized it. Yeah, his resemblance to Jeff was a little too eerie for my tastes. I'd have to do something to fix that.

"Dancing sounds yummy!" I said, putting an extra helping of stupid into my tone.

A few more drinks, some blows on the dice for luck, and a lot of banal conservation later found me acting nice and tipsy. It had been no effort at all for Tad the cad to lure me away from the tables, or so I let him believe. Standing outside his hotel room, we both knew that the only dancing he had in mind was between the sheets.

"Mind if I change into something more comfortable first?"

Really? He actually used that line? He was acting more like Jeff by the moment.

"Sure thing," I purred with a strategically placed slur.

"Why don't you come inside and wait."

I refrained from replying, "I thought you'd never ask." Far too cliché. Instead, I obediently followed him in.

Once inside, he shut the door and put his body between me and the exit as he stealthily tried to engage the privacy lock. Oh Tad, you bad boy, you.

"Hurry up," I said. "I can't wait to go out and... mmmmrph."

He leaned down without preamble and planted his mouth against mine. I acted a bit surprised before melting into it. Truth be told, he wasn't a bad kisser. Our tongues entwined and I tasted the alcohol on his breath as well as the lingering remnants of the toothpaste he'd obviously used before coming downstairs...Crest, if I wasn't mistaken. Superior vampire senses can be a real trip sometimes.

His heartbeat sped up and his scent turned musky. Tad was getting turned on, no doubt anticipating moving in for the kill. Pity - that was going to be my move.

Does he really deserve it?

The voice popped into my head unexpectedly and I paused in the middle of our game of tongue hockey. It was rare for my conscience to bother me, but it had been happening more frequently ever since Bill entered my life. Between his influence and the trip down memory lane I'd been experiencing ever since Christy walked into the office, I was having an actual crisis of vampiredom. What a concept.

Fine, I said to myself. *Let's give him a chance.* There were plenty of potential targets in this city, many of whom didn't look disturbingly like the man who had been the death of me.

I pulled back. "Hold on. What about dancing?"

"Dancing can wait." He pressed against me once more. His arms circled my waist and he steered me toward the queen-sized bed in the room. The bulge in his pants said he probably wasn't going to accept a friendly handshake before calling it a night.

"No," I stammered, trying to give him one last out. God, I must be going batty to be such a softy at my age. "Stop..."

"I don't think so," he said, his grin turning predatory. His hands moved up to grab hold of my arms in a grip that would've been painful had I not possessed several times his strength.

Oh well, never let it be said I didn't give him a chance.

He once more pressed against me, burying his mouth into mine. I put up a feeble attempt at a struggle, but he kept my arms pinned to my side. This was the part I loved best.

There's something about a predator reaching the apex of their supposed power that really puts an extra bit of spice into their blood. Mixed with the fear and confusion that followed, it was quite the intoxicating brew.

My date for the evening gave me a shove and I fell back, landing on the overly soft mattress. They build them with a little extra bounce in places like these, knowing that only a small percentage of the people staying there would actually be using them to sleep.

Tad was immediately atop me, forcing my legs

apart as he settled his weight to pin me down. He reached one hand up, grasped the top of my dress, and yanked it down, exposing my right breast.

I had to fight to suppress a giggle. I was half-tempted to let him finish what he was starting. I'd developed a bit of a taste for the rough stuff in the years since I'd been here. As frail as he was, Tad's aggression was a bit of a turn on. Sick, ain't it? But then, that's what we vamps are all about.

Unfortunately, he had to go and ruin it for both of us.

"You're not going anywhere."

Memories rushed in unbidden, and with that, Tad's fate was sealed.

13

1979

I lay there with only the thin sheet to cover me. I kept trying to come up with some excuse for my actions: too much drink; seeing Uncle Colin caught me off guard; it was the cocaine Jeff had produced once we were alone. That last one seemed plausible. After all, it typically wasn't my style.

The reality was it was all bullshit, a way for me to justify having done what I'd done. I'd left the club with Jeff at the end of my shift for the simple reason that he was drop dead gorgeous. Words flowed from his mouth like a fine wine, each sip intoxicating me far more than the watered down drinks I had downed.

Still, a part of me felt like a whore. I'd never before cheated on a boyfriend. Sure, I danced at the club, but that was purely financial...no emotional attachment required. There were a few disturbing holes in my memory, nights that I had no knowledge of, but I had managed to convince myself that there was nothing to worry about with those. I was young and on my own. Wasn't it natural to sometimes boogie a little too hard?

Yeah, I didn't quite buy it either. Fine, I never *willingly* cheated on a boyfriend before. Either you looked at it, Mark didn't deserve that. Sure, he wasn't much to look at, but then neither was I - no matter what the clients at the club might say. He was a sweet man, though. I wasn't in love with him, I had no delusions about that, but he was good to me.

At the same time, a voice in the back of my head reminded me, hadn't it been quite the difference - Jeff's hard body against mine? His chiseled form had been only half the thrill, though. He used it in ways that suggested he wasn't exactly inexperienced. Once he'd pressed his lips against mine, I'd been putty in his hands - his to do with as he pleased.

There were no two ways about it. It had been fun and, in the end, I'd had to bite down on Jeff's muscular shoulder to keep from crying out, afraid Mark's name would slip from my lips, even though he was far from my mind at the time. As I did, he let out a laugh as if something had been uproariously funny, but I was too far gone in the moment to protest.

"I like you, Lucinda," Jeff said, stepping out of the bathroom. Once more, I found my eyes drinking him in. He was one of those rare people who looked as good out of his clothes as in. "There's something about you..." He paused, seeming thoughtful for a moment. "I think I'd like to keep you." I giggled at the comment, thinking it was a joke. "You'll like New York."

"New York?"

"Yeah, the big city. Ever been there? It's a happening place."

"Nope. Maybe one day..."

"Not one day...now." He leaned over onto the bed and locked eyes with me. There was something in them I didn't like. I couldn't quite place it, but it made me feel uncomfortable. I unconsciously pulled the sheet up further on my body.

"It's like Colin said. I just recently took over my organization and it's growing again. I'm looking for people who'll fit in. I think you'll do nicely."

"I'm really not looking for another job."

"It's not a job offer." His eyes practically glittered. "Jobs are beneath us, as are the beetles that scurry under our feet performing them."

Goose bumps broke out on my skin. One moment, I was in post-coital bliss. The next, the temperature in the room seemed to drop twenty degrees. There was something overly predatory about the way he looked at me. I didn't like it one bit. It made me feel like a piece of meat.

Trying to keep my tone steady, I bunched up the covers around me and slid off the bed. "Listen, this has been fun, but I have a boyfriend. I can't just up and..."

"Not anymore you don't." As quick as a snake, he was in front of me. I actually jumped back a step. It was almost like magic. I'd never seen anyone move that fast.

"Did I scare you?"

"No," I lied, stepping past him. "Really, Jeff, that was cute and all, but..."

He grabbed my arm and spun me around to face him. I let out a yelp, but he appeared not to notice.

"About that name...none of my close friends call me that. They call me Night Razor."

"Night..."

"Yeah, and I think you and I are going to be really close from here on in."

His grip tightened. Tears sprang to my eyes as panic began to set in. How could I have missed it before? This guy was fucking crazy.

"Please let me go," I said in a small voice.

He flung me back onto the bed as if I was a rag doll. He tore the sheet off me and climbed atop, pinning my arms above my head. I tried to fight, but his grip was too strong. I couldn't even budge him.

"You're not going anywhere - ever again," he whispered.

I opened my mouth to scream, but it died in my throat as Jeff...Night Razor...changed. His eyes turned black as coal and his teeth elongated into cruel fangs, seemingly as sharp as daggers.

My sanity began to slip as he lowered his mouth toward me. Once he'd thrown me on the bed, I was sure I was about to be raped. I now saw that what he intended to do was far worse.

14

PRESENT DAY

Playtime was over. The smile on Tad's face turned to a look of confusion as I powered my way up and easily flipped us so that I was on top. I grabbed his wrists and pinned him. Confusion gave way to pain as I increased the pressure to the point where his bones cracked under my grasp.

He cried out - music to my ears.

"You took everything from me." I was still caught up in the memory. Oh well, the *faux pas* wouldn't matter in a moment.

Vaguely remembering that there was a method to my madness, I let his screams carry on for a moment longer. I wanted to make sure someone on the floor heard him.

I extended my fangs, threw Tad a wicked smile, and immediately buried my teeth into his neck before he could make another sound.

I'd love to tell you that I took just enough to satisfy myself, that it wasn't overkill, but that couldn't be farther from the truth. I drank my fill of Tad, and when I was done, continued tearing into him. Experienced vamps can control who they turn. I've been doing this for a while and had no intention of making a Tadpire. Even had I not, though, there was no way he would've risen again once I was finished with him.

His head was just barely still connected to the rest of him when the pounding started on the door. It was about fucking time. Either the creatures downstairs had already started whatever shenanigans they were up to, or the hotel staff was really slipping.

"Open up - security!"

"Just a minute," I called back sweetly. I stood and straightened my dress. It was more out of habit than anything. The outfit was completely and utterly soaked through with blood. It was gonna take a lot more than a trip to the dry cleaners to make this one wearable again. Oh well, I could afford another.

"Open this door immediately or we'll..."

I unlatched the lock, pulled it open, and stepped behind it. Two men rushed past into the room. One wore a suit, obviously management, and the other was a grunt. They stopped just inside, no doubt to admire my handiwork. While they gaped, I closed the door behind them.

The guard never stood a chance. I shattered his spine with my fist before he even realized I was there.

He dropped to his knees and keeled over. Eyes still blackened, I stepped forward.

The manager backed up a step, then slipped in some of Tad and fell on his ass. It was almost funny. I made a note to remember to laugh when this was all over. He pulled a walkie-talkie out. "Code sixty-six! I repeat, code sixty-six!"

Ah, that's what I was waiting for. Only the true bigwigs in this town knew of our existence, but security was always trained to deal with *oddities*. Anything that fell somewhere on the scale between *holy shit* and *what the fuck* would get a call sign of sixty-six. Other ears, non-human ones, continually monitored the feeds for just such a code.

Alas, that meant I still had some time left to kill. I stepped forward and knocked the radio from his hand, breaking his arm in the process.

Dragging him to his feet by his tie, I roughly pushed his head to the side and indulged myself in another drink. When it's fresh from the tap, might as well take all you can get - that's my motto.

As I sucked out his lifeblood, I had a moment to reflect how it was ironic that I'd been prepared to spare Tad, my would-be rapist, yet had never given these two men a chance. They'd only been doing their jobs, and I'd taken everything from them without a second thought.

Alas, blood is intoxicating. It tends to make us forget reason for a time. Even the most levelheaded vampire can become a shark at a feeding frenzy if the conditions are right. Sadly for them, with blood flowing freely and visions of Jeff still fresh in my mind, it was the perfect recipe for a massacre.

I waited patiently. The scent of blood still filled the air, but I was pretty darn full by then. That helped to dull the effect. Thus, I used the time to collect my thoughts again. The fun was over and done with. Now it was time for business...time to make formal contact. My original plan would have given us a chance to negotiate. This way, though, was bound to put Marlene and her minions in a tizzy.

At the very least, that was bound to be a shitload more fun.

In time, doors opened and feet shuffled about in the hall. I knew what it meant. Anyone who had been within earshot of my earlier violence, especially those who had phoned security, were being silenced in one way or another. Unknown to the human guards expected to use it, a code sixty-six often meant no witnesses.

I listened with both my ears and my mind. The next few minutes were very telling. Nothing out of the ordinary filtered through. That meant no compulsions. Whoever was in the cleanup crew wasn't very old. It took a vampire of considerable power to compel a human, especially one with anything resembling willpower. Hell, I could just barely do it. Anyone younger would have an equal chance of knocking themselves out if they even tried.

Finally, silence returned to the floor. I waited for a moment longer, then heard a sound right outside the door.

It was show time.

15

1979

I awoke with a start, gasping for breath as if I hadn't done so in far too long. I opened my eyes and immediately squeezed them shut as a wave of vertigo passed through me. The room seemed far too bright and insanely vivid, as if someone had repainted it in neon colors.

As I lay there, eyes closed, I raised a hand to massage my temples. I took a deep breath through my nose and my nostrils tingled. There was an odd coppery odor to the air...unpleasant, yet somewhat intoxicating at the same time. As I processed this, memories flooded into me...unpleasant ones of creatures with soulless eyes and nightmare teeth.

"Jeff!" I gasped before putting a hand over my mouth.

He'd...he'd...but that was insane.

I sat up and cracked my eyes open again, slowly this time. The world came back into focus in that same way as before, as if everything was in extra sharp contrast. It was weird. I'd never tried LSD, but my friends at the club had told me of experiences similar to this.

I remembered how Jeff had produced a vial of white powder and then helped himself to a line of it across my bare breasts. I was so caught up in the moment that I'd also indulged. At the time, it had turned me on wildly. Now I wondered what the hell had been in it. It had either been spectacularly good coke, or horrifically bad.

That had to be it. I was in the middle of a goddamned drug trip.

The whole mess with Jeff must've been some fucked up hallucination. There was no other explanation. Speaking of which, I looked about. He was nowhere to be seen.

"Hello?" I tentatively called out. My voice slurred a bit. Something about my mouth felt odd. Hell, my whole body felt...*off*.

No answer came. I was alone in the room.

"Son of a bitch had his way then left," I muttered, not entirely surprised. Served me right too, falling for his bullshit. "Congratulations, Lucinda. You've just been some dickhead's one-night stand. With your luck, you're probably pregnant." I let out a bitter laugh.

Wouldn't that be something? I'd left home, tired of listening to my father's bullshit insistence that women were meant to be barefoot and pregnant. Wouldn't it be ironic to return home in that state? I was sure that once Linda heard about it, she'd be twice the smug bitch she usually was.

I shook my head. I was getting way ahead of myself. Still, I didn't feel quite right. The room was still way too bright and now I found myself oddly hungry...very hungry, as a matter of fact.

Oh no, maybe I was pregnant after all. Tears welled up in my eyes as I glanced down at myself, imagining my body with a belly big with child.

That's when I saw all the blood.

It was all over the bed and all over me. How the hell hadn't I noticed it? As I stared at the previously white bed sheet, an insane urge came over me. I wanted to put it into my mouth and suck it dry. Hell, I even found myself leaning toward it before realizing what I was doing.

Jesus Christ, what the hell did he drug me with?

Or did he?

I remembered the nightmare. Him pinning me down, forcing himself on me just before his eyes turned black. The horrific sensation of having my throat ripped out, of trying to scream, but being unable to make any noise above a pained gurgle. After that, it had all gone black.

I immediately reached up to touch my neck, fearing that I'd feel the bloody grizzle of torn flesh. *That made no sense*, a small voice in my head insisted - after all, I was still able to speak. There was no wound, not even any pain. It did feel oddly tacky, though. I pulled my hands away and looked down.

Unsurprisingly, they were covered in blood. I was forced to assume it was mine.

A scream bubbled up in my throat. I quickly cupped my hands over my mouth, knowing that kind of ruckus would attract attention. If found in this manner, I would be questioned...hell, I might even be arrested. A girl abandoned in a hotel room wasn't exactly out of the ordinary in this city. The blood, though, was bound to attract some attention.

The blood...

Against all good sense, I began licking my fingers.

I should have been horrified. I mean, who wouldn't be? Sane people didn't do things like that...not even in this city. Instead, my body shuddered as if in the grip of an orgasm - a pretty damn intense one, I might add. Before I knew it, I was sucking on my fingers as if they were covered in the nectar of the gods. I couldn't stop myself. I had to get every last drop. I had to...

"Ow!"

I pulled my hand from my mouth to find a nasty puncture on one finger. I stared as blood welled from it for a moment, then my eyes opened wide in surprise as I watched the wound close.

That did it. The spell was broken. Before I found myself licking the sheets clean, I bounded out of the bed, my body feeling surprisingly nimble. I walked into the bathroom and turned on the light.

The reflection in the mirror was me...yet not me. Blood covered my still naked torso, but that wasn't the worst of it. The Lucinda that stared back at me had the same eyes and teeth as Jeff right before his attack.

I hadn't just imagined a nightmare. I was living one.

I needed to get out of there. Thankfully, enough rational thought remained to know that I had to be smart about it. A naked girl, covered in blood and screaming down the hall wasn't subtle, even in the City of Sin.

Resisting the crazed urges to yell, break stuff, or run, I quickly turned on the shower - hot as it would go - and stepped in.

The water should have scalded me, but I felt no pain. Must have been shock or something. I didn't quite know how that worked, but my father had been a fan of *Marcus Welby, M.D.* and I'd seen enough episodes to sort of have an idea. Whatever the case, I stayed under the spray of water until no traces of blood remained.

Stepping out, I dried myself with a towel, grateful that no tinges of pink seemed to stain it. The room still appeared overly sharp, but I felt more like myself. Though a part of me didn't want to look again, I wiped some of the steam from the mirror and risked another glimpse. Amazingly enough, the nightmare version of me was gone - if it had ever been real to begin with. My own green eyes stared back. I dared a smile and the same grin that had always been there reflected back.

It was so odd. I found myself thinking of the *Twilight Zone* episodes I had watched as a child. Somehow, I had found myself there. A disturbing thought, considering many didn't exactly end on a happy note. A part of me wondered what other unpleasant surprises awaited.

I stepped out of the bathroom and glanced toward the bed. Sure enough, the gore remained. It hadn't all been a hallucination. That was enough for me. Without further hesitation, I gathered my clothes - thankfully, blood free - dressed, and got the hell out of there.

16

PRESENT DAY

Things went about as expected. Upon entering, two vampires - relative newbs, judging by the nervous way they held themselves - took stock of the scene. They tried to play it tough, but did a shit job of it.

"What the fuck do you think you're doing?" one of them growled at me. He was a big guy, nearly six and a half feet tall. He wore an off-the-shelf suit and sported your typical tough-guy buzz cut. If I had to guess, I'd say he was either a former security grunt or bouncer. He held himself as if he were used to getting his way by virtue of his size, but there was something a bit subdued about his gruff demeanor. I'd have been willing to bet that he'd learned one of the more important lessons the supernatural world had to offer - size didn't mean shit when it came to power.

I indulged in a smile. For petite girls like myself, becoming a vampire was a true equalizer - far more effective than any law or doctrine ever could be. Most teen girls get stars in their eyes about vampires because they get caught up in the eternal love bullshit Hollywood seems to be dishing out as of late. The reality was that if there was any reason to be enamored with joining the ranks of the undead, it was because it meant a life of never having to fear guys like Tad ever again.

I stared up at Buzz Cut, experiencing a brief flashback to the first time I'd met a Sasquatch, the ancient enemies of the vampire world. Sadly, for the big guy in front of me, he was about three feet short of being as intimidating.

"I asked you a question," he huffed. I held his gaze, ignoring his partner, who appeared to be taking a wait and see approach. While the big goon might play the alpha male, the other seemed to have the advantage of a brain in his head.

The battle of wills lasted just a few moments. I grinned and took a sudden step forward. The vamp in front of me reacted just enough to tell us both who the winner was here.

I glanced casually at the gore around me. "I *think* I was enjoying my vacation until you showed up."

"You're that broad from New York, right?"

"I'm that *coven master* from New York. I suggest you remember that." My icy tone had the desired effect on Buzz Cut, but he still wasn't quite ready to admit he'd lost this game of chicken. The poor guy must've had a small dick or something.

"How do you know I'm not the coven master here?"

I let out a laugh. "This is Marlene's territory. Last I checked, she was prettier than you."

Had we both been mortal, he'd have probably put me through a wall for that remark. Alas, we weren't, and he no doubt knew that if he tried it, he'd end the day with a bunch of cigarette butts sticking from his remains. Fortunately, his partner picked that moment to step in. "Please forgive us, coven master Sally." Ooh, he'd done his homework, too.

I turned to face him. Tall, wiry, and with thinning blonde hair, he'd been turned a bit later in life than most others, but it had served to instill upon him a modicum of tact. He'd be one to watch.

"I'd like to request that you come with us, if you would."

"And should I choose not to?"

"You know we can't make you."

Yeah, he was definitely one to watch. His no-neck buddy would be lucky to live past the next decade, but this one was a survivor. One could always tell another.

I had every intention of going with them, but that didn't mean I had to make it easy. I sent the smarter of the two to my room to fetch something else for me to wear. It wouldn't do to walk even to the service elevator looking like I did, and I didn't trust Buzz Cut to not fuck it up.

While that happened, I stepped into the shower to clean up a bit. I left the door unlocked, practically daring the big goon to try his luck. Sadly, he didn't opt for an early death. I made a mental note to up my opinion of him a notch as I toweled off.

When the thin guy got back, I took my sweet time making myself presentable. When I finally stepped back out into the hall, you'd have never guessed the carnage I'd caused had ever occurred.

Their families will never know what happened to them.

Goddamnit! If Bill ever returned, I was going to punch his lights out for infecting me with his fucking morality. It was starting to get annoy...

I stopped in my tracks. Buzz Cut bumped into me, but I barely noticed.

If Bill ever returned.

It was the first time I'd seriously considered that he might not be coming back.

A glimmer of sadness crept into my consciousness at the thought. It was only a small sliver, but for someone like me, who was used to suppressing any feelings that didn't involve contempt, it was practically a tidal wave of emotion.

"Let's move it. We've wasted enough time." A meaty hand fell upon my shoulder.

It was a big mistake.

I grabbed Buzz Cut's hand and twisted. He cried out in surprise and I spun, bringing his arm up behind him.

"You bitch, I'll..."

Crack I snapped two of his fingers without a second thought. He opened his mouth to scream, but before it escaped I put one hand on his shoulder and shoved him face first into the wall, denting it nice and proper.

The thin one took a step toward us, but I stopped him with a glare. In the past year, I'd killed two master vampires, tangled with Templar knights, and faced off against a ten-foot monster ape. These assholes were less than nothing to me, and I was sure as hell going to make sure they knew it if they pushed me.

"We should probably get moving," thin guy suggested, then started walking again.

"Lead the way," I said, following.

"Barlow," he called back, "straighten yourself out and catch up."

"Barlow?" I asked. "He calls himself Barlow?"

"It's from a Stephen Ki..."

"I know what it's from. Jeez. Not even trying, is he?"

He risked a glance back at me and grinned. Yeah, I liked this guy. I almost found myself hoping I wouldn't have to kill him.

17

At this hour, the sky was starting to lighten in the east. I glanced in that direction and saw dark clouds looming on the horizon, the occasional flash of light illuminating them. Though the wind was against it, a few moments of observation made it clear the storm was moving in this direction...fuck! I had the sinking sensation we were about to be slammed with the same supernatural storm Christy and I had flown through the day before. That had potential to add a new level of weird to my plans. Even so, it appeared to still be a few hours off. The sun would be up long before then.

Pandora's Box was on the edge of the city, purposefully placed with one side looking out over the desert. There was a lot of open space beyond in which to make someone disappear if the need arose, which with vampires, it often did. If we used the car that was now pulling in for us, we'd be lucky to make it there before the first rays of sun illuminated the tops of the casinos. It would be cutting it close, especially as there was another way.

The underground of Las Vegas was nearly as vast as that of New York City. Sewers, old drain tunnels, and the like formed an immense network that spanned the width of the city. They allegedly went pretty deep, too, albeit that was one rumor that, even as a vampire, I wasn't privy to the truth behind. I'd only utilized them during my last days as a resident here, and only then to stay out of the sunlight.

Still, they were well known in the vampire community. Vegas was a city that tended to frown upon the homeless. Thus, many made their way underground to eke out whatever means of survival they could. Down there, they were safe from police harassment. What the denizens of Vegas's underbelly didn't realize was that this protection from the law was purposeful, courtesy of Marlene. It was quite brilliant, really, both a safe haven from the sun and a giant larder full of tasty treats that wouldn't be missed.

"We're not using the tunnels?" I asked, more curious that anything. Hoping I'd get dusted by the rising sun was a stupid plan for even newbs like my escorts. Besides, had Marlene meant to make an example of me that way, she'd have sent some heavier backup. Neither Barlow nor his partner, who went by the deliciously ordinary name of Steve, were a threat to me.

The two shared a glance. Something about my question made them uncomfortable.

"We're sticking topside," Steve said. "Marlene

didn't want you to get nervous." It was a pathetic lie. What vampire worth their salt would get even remotely nervous down in the dark? If anything, the opposite would be true.

Fortunately, I wasn't a fucking idiot. I just didn't need to let my two tour guides know that.

"I appreciate her concern," I said, adding a little attitude. "It's about fucking time I got shown a little courtesy. Now don't go and ruin it by saying you expect me to sit up front."

As we'd approached the club's gleaming exterior, I'd felt a twinge in my gut as if the blood of Tad and the security manager weren't agreeing with me. That was stupid of course, but not as stupid as letting the memory of coming back...coming home, so to speak....unnerve me, as it was.

I stepped from the limo and was ushered to the side door. The car had parked on the west side of the club, affording us the protection of being in the building's shadow. That was odd. Pandora's Box had an underground parking lot like the northeast vampire HQ in Boston. One didn't ask visiting guests, especially ones of rank, to make a mad dash to keep out of the weather. Was it, perhaps, a purposeful insult, or something else?

The building had changed in the ensuing thirty some-odd years. The signage was updated and the outer façade was less gaudy than I remembered, no doubt a result of the seventies ending and people coming to their senses. Ninety-five percent of the business was on the up and up...at least as far as Vegas was concerned. It was the remaining five percent that was the killer. Most girls showed up, danced, made their money, then went home. Only the truly unlucky ones were singled out.

For perhaps the first time this trip, my thoughts truly turned toward Tom's sister. I didn't know her from a hole in the wall, aside from a picture Christy had shown me on the flight over. At the same time, I felt a connection to her. Hadn't we both known people we trusted who weren't quite what they seemed?

"And how are your studies going, my dear Lucinda?"

"Not so well, Uncle Colin."

"I'm sorry to hear that. You're a very bright girl. Lots of potential."

"I don't know. Dad doesn't..."

"Your father and I have been friends for years and I greatly respect his vision, but I think he's oddly blind when it comes to his own family."

"You think so?"

"I know so."

"Thanks. Hey, Uncle Colin..."

"Yes, my dear?"

"Can you keep a secret?"

"Of course."

"Okay, well, I haven't told anyone else this, but I'm thinking of leaving."

"Leaving?"

"Well, yeah. Graduation is almost here, and Linda is pressuring me to join her down at the dress shop. Says it's a proper place for us to work."

"But you don't agree?"

"No. I want..."

"More?"

"Yes. I know what Daddy says, but I..."

"I think it's a good idea. You should get out there, see the world."

The interior hadn't changed as much as I'd have thought. It had been upgraded, new lighting, the works, but the layout was still the same. The main stage dominated the place, with several smaller stages off to the side. The bar still ran the length of the eastern wall. I couldn't see them from this vantage point, but far left of the stage was an entrance to the back, where the private rooms were. A set of stairs ran up from there to the second floor where the *special* guests were entertained...the ones that, even now, I couldn't quite remember.

Anger filled me at the thought of the gaps in my memory. Who knows what happened up there? The only thing I was sure of was that I hadn't been killed, although that was small comfort. Jeff had seen to that little detail.

"Hello?"

"Hi, Uncle Colin."

"Lucinda?"

"Yeah, it's me."

"Where in the world are you, my dear? Your parents have been worried sick."

"That's why I called. I didn't want to...well, you know. But I was hoping you could let them know I was okay."

"Of course. But you didn't answer me. Where are you?"

"Promise not to tell?"

"I'm somewhat insulted. Did I not give you my word before you left? Have I not kept it? As long as you're safe, why would I betray you now?"

"I'm sorry. You're right. Okay, well this is kind of weird, but I'm living in Las Vegas."

"Vegas?"

"Oh, don't be worried. I'm not doing anything bad. I'm just waiting tables."

"Gainful employment, to be sure, but perhaps a little beneath you."

"I'm surviving. That's the important part."

"Indeed it is. But at the same time, I have friends there. I could give you their number and I'm sure they'd be happy to..."

"No, it's okay. I don't want to be a bother."

"It wouldn't be a bother at all."

"Thanks, but I don't want you to go to that trouble. I'm...happy. I'm making it."

"On your own, too."

"Yeah, there's that."

"Very well, but perhaps I'll put the word out for them to keep their eyes open for you regardless."

I'd since wondered whether it was indeed a coincidence that I was recruited for Pandora's Box. After all, Vegas didn't exactly have a shortage of attractive women. In a place like this you probably couldn't throw a rock without hitting a few potentials. Considering that my relationship with Colin had been somewhat strained ever since the day I was killed, it wasn't all too surprising that he hadn't ever been forthcoming with an answer. That was okay. I'd get the truth out of him one day.

For now, the club was quiet. The doors closed to the public at five a.m. The last girls would have left a short while after; some to go home, others to less savory destinations. The living wouldn't return to the premises until the afternoon to prep for the evening ahead. But the living weren't really my concern at that moment.

"Marlene's waiting in her office," Barlow growled, his voice sounding normal again. Guess his busted face had healed. He started walking and I found myself actually following.

For just a second, it seemed the years melted away. I was once again a naïve girl, scared and all too willing to jump at the say so of those I considered my betters.

It only lasted for a second, though. I veered to the left and planted myself in a chair at one of the tables.

"What are you doing?" the shaved ape asked. God, some people just didn't learn their lesson.

"You know," I said idly, pulling a tube of lipstick out of my bag for a touch up, "I'm starting to get tired of you, but I'm in a generous mood today so I'll explain things slowly." I didn't look up, speaking as I went about my task. "I don't work for Marlene, and I sure as shit don't work for you. I'm your superior in *every* conceivable way."

I put the tube back, extended the claws on my right hand, and casually placed it upon the table. I began to carve lazy circles in the wood with my index finger, the loud scraping echoing in the quiet club. "For your sake, I highly suggest you remember that the next time you open your fucking mouth. Now go tell Marlene that her guest is waiting for her."

I sat back and dragged my finger across the now scarred table. "Oh, and get me a drink while I'm waiting...something fruity would be nice."

18

"What do you call this?" I took another sip. The place wasn't quite as empty as it initially appeared. That wasn't surprising - I had smelled the presence of other vampires. Pandora's Box was a coven HQ, after all.

Following my little show of strength, Barlow had walked off in a huff - but at least it was a respectful huff. Steve had made a subtle nod, at which point another vamp had walked out and taken a place behind the bar.

"That's a Sandy Corpse," the bartender said. "It's a Sex on the Beach with a splash of fermented O-positive."

"Well, it's nummy," I replied in a chipper tone. I wasn't just bullshitting either. I made a mental note to recruit a good bartender for Village Coven. Why hadn't I thought of that before? Must be the stress of recent times. When all of this bullshit was over and done with - *if* it ever was - I'd have to work on putting a little class back into my coven.

"I see our little Lucinda has come back to us."

The voice was cordial enough with its ever-so-slight French accent, but my skin crawled nevertheless. I took one more sip of the drink, enjoying the taste for a moment longer - anticipating the flavor of bile that would no doubt soon be entering my mouth. I put it down and looked up.

Marlene stood just inside the entrance of the room. She was average height, full-figured, and with auburn hair. She'd probably be considered plus-sized by the silly standards of the modern world, but it was hard to deny her beauty. Even the most die-hard fan of stick figure models would be hard pressed to turn her down.

I'd heard that she used to turn the heads of royalty back in the French court, and it was easy to see why. She was dressed conservatively, considering her position, looking more likely to officiate a marketing meeting than peddle the flesh of others. Her outfit did nothing, though, to suppress the feline grace with which she moved, carrying herself with an authority that few of her rank could convey. She was definitely the alpha female in this pride of lions.

Coven master or not, most vampires my age would've been wise to give her a wide berth when she entered the room. Pity for her I wasn't most vampires.

"Lucinda's been dead for a long time," I said, partially surprised at the calmness of my voice. A small part of me had been afraid that the girl I had once been might come screaming out of my subconscious at the first sight of her. I was glad to see that she stayed put in whatever dark closet she'd retreated to all those years ago.

"I had heard about Jeff's silly rule. I thought with him gone..."

"He was a fucking idiot," I interrupted, "but there was some logic behind his decree...casting off our old selves so that we could begin anew."

She raised an eyebrow at my reply, although it was hard to tell whether she was insulted or bemused. With no further preamble, she took a seat opposite me at the table. It was, no doubt, her subtle way of reminding me whose turf we were on.

"Sally Sunset it is, then."

"Just Sally. Even I have my limits."

"Very well. So, *Sally*," she began, rolling my name around in her mouth as if tasting it, "my men have told me that you made quite the mess over at the Grand."

I shrugged. "I was letting off some steam. Been a while since I've given myself a vacay."

"Is that so?"

"It is."

"It's highly unusual for a coven master to enter my domain without visiting me first. I have to say, I was slightly insulted to think you'd fly in here for a few days and leave without saying hi."

"Well, these are unusual times."

Her eyes flashed angrily at that for some reason. "Yes, speaking of which, how is the Freewill I've heard so much about?"

"He's definitely not what you'd expect."

"So I've been told," she sniffed haughtily. Something about the subject of Bill was setting her off. I wondered if it was base jealousy. Wouldn't be the first time I'd seen it. There were quite a few who weren't overly happy at Village Coven's increased status as a result of being the birthplace of the vampire race's legendary warrior - even if he was about as intimidating as an angry kitten.

"But where are my manners?" she added. "You were one of my best girls and it's wonderful to see how far you've managed to come. This should be a time of celebration." I bristled ever so slightly at the *best girls* remark, but kept my demeanor pleasant, curious to see where this was going. "My men tell me you've already fed well this day, but I was hoping you'd indulge me and share a quick drink with your former master."

"Employer."

"Excuse me?"

"I worked for you. I was never a part of your coven."

"A matter of semantics. I like to think of all my people, turned or not, as part of the family." She let out a melodic laugh then snapped her fingers. "Barlow, if you'd be so kind." The goon obeyed and left the room like the good dog he was. I managed to suppress a smirk. It must drive the macho asshole nuts to be reduced to being a gofer for the fairer sex.

I ran my finger over the wet rim of my glass, producing a quick hum of sound. "Thanks, but they took care of me before you entered."

"Nonsense. I wouldn't dream of letting you leave without cracking open a fresher vintage."

Fresher?

Barlow reentered with a girl in tow, a human. The dim light of the club did nothing to keep my vampire eyes from registering her face. Though she'd been clad in more than just a bra and panties in the photo I'd seen, there was no mistaking Tom's sister.

What the hell? My eyes opened wide in surprise. There was no way this was a coincidence.

"What's the matter, Lucinda?" Marlene asked as she leaned toward me. She smiled a wide predatory grin as if she were a cat who had just discovered a mouse in her presence. "You look like you've seen a ghost."

Fuck me! I'd obviously been made, so there was no reason to continue this charade. Barlow and the bartender, fuck if that didn't sound like a bad sitcom title, were too far away to do much, but Steve was right behind me. I grabbed my glass and squeezed until it shattered, momentarily regretting wasting the rest of my drink, then flung the shards of broken glass back over my shoulder

Not bothering to wait for his reaction, I shoved my table forward into Marlene, sending her off balance, then reached over to the table next to us and tore one of the legs clean off. I stood and raised the makeshift stake, the entire affair taking perhaps no more than three seconds.

"*SIT DOWN!!*"

Which was apparently at least two and a half seconds too long. Oh well, I'd figured it for a long shot anyway. Can't say I didn't try.

My butt immediately planted itself back in the chair.

"*DROP IT!!* And let's continue this conversation like civilized adults."

A vampire as old as Marlene would be a master at compulsion. Despite my age and the defenses I'd built up against it, she was still far too powerful. I obeyed like she knew I would.

"That's better," she said, composing herself. I looked around and noticed the bartender and Barlow right where they'd been. My senses told me that Steve was likewise back in position, albeit perhaps a little wetter than he had been. Either way, they'd all obviously been well aware of the outcome. On paper, Marlene and I might be the same rank, but in actual practice there was quite a gap between us.

Interestingly enough, Kara was unfazed as well. She continued walking toward our table. I wasn't stupid enough to think she was that cool of a customer. If she shared even a fraction of the same genetic code as her brother, that would be near impossible. That being said, Tom had proven himself to be quite susceptible to Christy's mind fuckings. The calm, almost glassy-eyed stare in her eyes as she approached pretty much confirmed that like her brother, Kara was a prime candidate for compulsion.

"Have a seat, my dear," Marlene cooed. Barlow dragged over one of the chairs from the table I'd broken and Kara sat down. She was a pretty thing. Pity she was a fucking dumbass.

"Looks like I owe someone a wager," Marlene said. I cocked my head to the side, confused. She explained, "I always thought you were a smart one, Lucinda. I figured at the very least it might take three, maybe more, tries to lure you out here. Sad to say either I was wrong about you, or your traveling companion - the one currently skulking outside - was quite persuasive. Stephen, take some men and invite her in. Be careful, though. I have a sneaking suspicion she's more than meets the eye."

19

I gave an easy shrug. "Guess my thrall was a bit overeager."

"Thrall?" The doubt was obvious in her voice.

"Of course. If I'd just brought her as a snack, I wouldn't have had to party earlier. Do you mind, by the way? My ass is starting to go a little numb."

Marlene released a breath and her concentration slackened. "Very well. Just behave yourself or next time I'll make sure that's the least of your worries."

"Point taken." I shifted in my seat, finding a more comfortable position.

I heard movement behind me. I turned my head to find Christy being escorted into the building. Three men surrounded her. Judging by their lack of coverings, I guessed they were human...most likely the daytime bouncers. I also had little doubt they were what I claimed Christy was: thralls - weak-willed people given multiple deep compulsions over time, gradually having a cumulative effect until they were beholden to a particular vampire or coven. It was a subtle art that required a lot of concentration, something that, in all honesty, I'd never tried.

The men marched Christy up to the table and remained next to her. I couldn't help but notice she wasn't asked to sit. Her eyes immediately turned toward our quarry.

"Kara?"

I let out a deep sigh. "Way to go, Mata Hari."

"You say that as if the cat wasn't already out of the bag, Lucinda," Marlene purred, sounding extra smug. She turned to Christy, then glanced back at me. "Cute. If she wasn't hiding her true form, I might offer her a job."

What the...? "True form?"

"You can drop the glamour, witch."

"She's not a..."

"Oh, please. I smelled her the second she walked through the door."

Before parting ways in the casino, I'd discussed my plan with Christy. Outside of the glamour, she wasn't to use any obvious magic - like, say, disintegrating someone - unless necessary. Though the existence of mages was known amongst vampire-kind, not too many of us state-side had been exposed to them. Before recent events, the surviving wizards and witches of the world had been keeping a very low profile, having been all but wiped out just a few centuries ago. I'd been counting on Marlene not being familiar with them. Christy would, thus, be our ace in the hole when the time came to get nasty.

She had played her part perfectly - keeping an eye on the casino exits and following me when I left - all with the intention of being caught. She hadn't done anything to give herself away, which meant Marlene was somehow in the know.

"How..."

"I said to drop the glamour," Marlene snarled.

Before either of us could react, one of the goons plowed his fist into Christy's stomach, doubling her over.

Once more, a flicker of emotion passed through me where there should have been nothing more than an icy center. I found myself rising, ready to dole out some hurt to her attacker.

"Don't try it unless you want me to convince you otherwise again."

Her last compulsion was still a fresh memory. I forced an expression of neutrality back onto my face and made myself comfortable again.

Christy let out a whimper of pain. Her form shimmered as the glamour dropped and she filled out her dress.

Marlene sniffed again. "A pregnant witch, no less. You do run with an interesting crowd these days, Lucinda."

"I can't help but notice you keep calling me that."

"And I'm sure you can't help but notice that I'm in a position to call you whatever I so please."

I gritted my teeth and took it, despite wanting to smash hers in. "How'd you know about her? I didn't think many of our kind..."

"You silly girl, this is Vegas. Half the stage magicians on the strip are the real deal and most of them are regular customers."

Oh. Yeah, I guess that'd do it. It really had been a long time since I'd been here.

Marlene's focus immediately turned back to Christy. In a flash, her claws extended and she placed them at the still stupefied Kara's throat. "Be good."

I glanced down and saw an angry red glow had begun to surround Christy. She looked at me, hot death flashing in her eyes, and I gave my head the subtlest shake I could. Powerful as she was, this was a losing battle...for now. God help this place if anything happened to her baby, though.

Fortunately, she still had her wits about her. The glow persisted for a moment longer before subsiding.

Marlene retracted her claws, but kept one hand on Kara's shoulder. "That's a good pet. A woman in your condition shouldn't get herself too worked up. Now keep quiet and let the superior species converse."

That's one thing about most vamps - when they have the upper hand, they'll just keep on pouring salt into the wound. I usually found it to be an endearing trait, but I could see how it might get on one's nerves.

"Are we about finished with the games, Marlene?" I had a feeling if she pushed Christy enough, the poor girl would let loose with everything she had. I kinda preferred not sitting next to her when that happened. "Let's cut the bullshit. You obviously know why we're here. What do you want for the girl?"

"Ooh, so we've moved on from posturing to negotiating, have we? Fine, I'll play along. I'm sure you'll appreciate that I hold all the cards, so my price might be a bit inflated."

"Are you going to wait for me to die of old age, or are you going to name it?"

"I don't think old age is going to be a problem for you, child. First, though, tell me what this girl is to you."

"She's nothing."

"If she was nothing, you wouldn't be here."

True enough. "She's important to the witch."

"We're getting closer, but I'd say we're still not there. Tell you what - I'll give you one more try. Give me a straight answer, or I'll gut this pretty little thing here."

She meant it. I knew what a vamp of Marlene's age was capable of. Even if Christy somehow managed to nuke this place, she still wouldn't be fast enough to keep Kara's innards from spilling onto the floor.

"Fine," I said through gritted teeth. "I know her brother and kind of owe him one. This is me squaring my debts."

"You know," a voice called from behind us, "it's funny to hear you say that, when you owe so much more to others."

Christy and I turned our heads to watch the newcomer step from the shadows. I had been so focused on what was happening around me that I hadn't heard anyone else enter.

"You son of a bitch!" Christy spat. "Is this how you repay Kara's love? You drag her here to this den of wolves?"

I could only stare, my mouth agape as she continued her tirade. Earlier, Marlene had said I looked as if I'd seen a ghost. Now I really was seeing one.

"Mark?"

20

1979

I raced through the still dark streets, trying to get as far from the nightmare I'd left behind as possible. With each moment, it felt more and more like a bad dream, but with each passing step, the guilt began to weigh on me.

By the time I reached the edge of the Strip, I'd half-convinced myself that the whole affair had been a bad dream brought on by my subconscious. In some ways, Jeff was a monster, but he hadn't flashed a set of fangs and killed me. That was stupid. Obviously, the cocaine mixed with the inherent guilt of having cheated on Mark had done a real job on me.

I stopped in my tracks, realizing I needed to see him. Whether it was to confess and beg forgiveness or just to be with him, enjoying the normalcy of our lives, I wasn't sure. I'd cross that bridge when I came to it.

It was sometime after four a.m. He'd be home, most likely asleep unless he had the breakfast shift today - I couldn't quite remember his schedule. My head was still fuzzy and I was getting hungry. Hopefully he wouldn't mind if I snuck something from the refrigerator of the small apartment he rented.

A few catcalls rang out as I turned the corner to his street. I looked and saw some drunken tourists whistling and waving at me. One, wearing a gaudy floral print shirt, pointed a finger toward his crotch.

Fuckers! They'd be hard pressed to whistle once I had torn their throats out...

What the hell? Did I actually consider *killing* those people just for being assholes? As if I even could. Still, that was weird. For just one small second, an overpowering rage bubbled up inside of me. Combined with the hunger eating away at my midsection, it was oddly overpowering.

I needed to get my head on straight. Fuck my job. I'd call Marlene later today and tell her I was sick. After that, maybe I'd contact Uncle Colin and let him know what kind of person his friend was. He'd probably be cross with me, but I had faith that he wouldn't associate with someone like that if he knew their true nature.

At last! The squat building where Mark lived came into sight. I took a step, then nearly doubled over as my stomach cramped up. It felt like my organs were getting ready to digest themselves. I needed to get something inside of me and fast. I couldn't understand it. Sure, I'd only had a salad for dinner the night before, but that wasn't different from most days. I wasn't a big fan of meat and had the feeling too many dishes of pasta wouldn't be amenable to my current job.

Maybe it was the drugs again. Did cocaine speed up your metabolism? I had no idea. I was nothing more than a dabbler at best.

It was only then that I realized I could make out every little detail of the building. Come to think of it, how could I have seen the shirt on that tourist? On the Strip, that was easy. It was never dark there. Once past the casinos, though, the glitz petered off. Hell, here on Mark's street, it was downright gloomy, yet I could see everything as if the sun was shining high in the sky.

My stomach growled again. I hurried on, opening my purse and digging out the key that Mark had given me some months back. He'd been dropping subtle hints about moving in together, but I'd been pretending to ignore it. Now, though, racing to be with him, I wondered if perhaps I'd been hasty. Maybe this ordeal was a wakeup call for me. I might not love him, but he'd never hurt me...maybe that was enough.

I let myself in, not bothering to turn on the light. His apartment stood before me in perfect clarity. My stomach cramped again. Food was my top priority.

"Lu? Is that you, darling?" Mark called from the bedroom. Immediately, all thoughts of the kitchen fled my mind. It was strange, but suddenly I needed him more than anything.

The entire apartment was awash in his smell. I took another breath, letting his scent fill me. I licked my lips, feeling a minor prick of pain as I did so, but barely noticed it.

"Lu?"

"I'm here," I whispered, kicking off my shoes. It was only a few steps to his tiny bedroom and I practically tore my dress off heading there. My need for him was overpowering. How could I have strayed? What could I have possibly seen in Jeff? The hell with Pandora's Box and everything else in this godforsaken town. I was never leaving Mark's side again.

"You're up early," he replied groggily as I entered his bedroom. "Is something wro..."

"No," I replied, tearing the sheets from atop him.

I straddled his hips, leaned down, and plunged my tongue into his mouth. Our bodies pressed together and his heart beat loud and strong through his skin.

He pulled back from my kiss for just a moment. "Whoa, Lu, you're ice cold. Been hanging out in a freezer all night? You might want to tell them to turn down the AC at..."

"Enough." I urgently pressed against him again. He smelled so good. His pulse raced as he became more excited, not that I needed anything to be able to tell - he was definitely responding to my attention. I crushed his mouth with mine, wishing us to be together as never before.

"Mmmrph!" He again pulled back from me. "Ow! What the hell, Lu? You got a razor blade in your mouth?"

The smell of blood filled my nostrils...*his* blood.

He started to gently guide me off of him. "I love it when you're aggressive, but maybe we should..."

I snarled and grasped his arms. My nails dug into his skin, and I easily overpowered him.

"Jesus Christ! What are you do..."

I didn't hear anything further. The scent of him, the sound of his heartbeat, the taste of him still in my mouth - it all filled me with an animalistic need. A small part of me realized what was happening and tried to cry out, but it was too late. When I pressed myself against Mark again, it was teeth first.

I drank in great swallows, enjoying the ambrosia as it flowed into my mouth in spurts. It was incredible. All at once, everything unpleasant in my life receded into complete unimportance. How could something taste so good? I had never in my life imagined anything so wonderful.

I took another swallow and shuddered as the equivalent of a dozen orgasms racked my body. My other times with Mark had been good, but never so satis...

Wait...Mark?

I seemed to remember something about him. Hadn't I been intent on joining him in bed? Perhaps, but that had been before. Now there was nothing but the blood. Full as I was, I found myself hoping it would never stop.

Sadly, though, it didn't last. What had been a

fountain slackened into a tiny trickle, weakly pumping as the heart behind it slowed.

...Heart?

I sat up, reluctantly pulling my face away from the wound I had created. Almost instantly, the euphoria receded as I saw the now vacant eyes of my lover.

"Mark?" I asked weakly. "Mark?" I gave his shoulder a shake, but there was no response. The flesh I'd torn with my teeth was the only answer I would be given.

21

I was completely speechless, torn between the sight of Mark standing there and the realization that he'd been the one to lure Kara away from her home. Had Bill been present, he'd have probably marked the occasion with a wiseass comment. I wished he were - whatever he said would, no doubt, have spurred me out of my shock.

"Now this is just delicious," Marlene purred, but she might as well have been miles away for all the attention I paid her.

I stood up, half expecting another compulsion to be shot my way, but none came. I stepped forward and took in the sight of him. He was dressed differently, far smarter than when I'd known him. His hair was similarly styled. He was no male model, but I had to admit, he cleaned up pretty well. If I'd had my current sense of fashion back then, I could've worked with this.

The differences seemed to go deeper than just

appearances, though. The shy man I'd known was gone. Mark carried himself with a swagger that suggested he was used to getting what he wanted. I could see how a girl like Kara might be taken in by him. It was amazing what a little bit of attitude could do for a person.

I stopped in front of him and he grinned, his teeth long and sharp.

"How?" I asked.

His answer came in the form of a fist rocketing into my face. I flew back and shattered the table Marlene was still seated at.

I found myself staring, dazed, up at the lights. He had a heck of a left hook.

"You were sloppy, love," he said, entering into my field of vision.

"Leave her alone!"

"I will caution you to stay out of this, witch," Marlene warned. "My tolerance for your existence will not extend toward interfering in our private affairs."

"It's okay, Christy." I spat out a wad of blood and pushed myself to my elbows.

"Sally, are you sure..."

"Sally, is it?" Mark scoffed. "I'd heard you were going by a new moniker. Not exactly what I'd have chosen. Reminds me of that actor from *All in the Family*. You remember watching that together, right?"

"How are you here?"

"It's like Mark said, child," Marlene replied. "You were sloppy. But then, you were sloppy about a great many things back in those days."

1979

I stepped out into the street to get away from the scene of my crime.

Oh, God...Mark! He'd been a good man. He didn't deserve what I'd done to him. What kind of monster had I become?

Almost as if fate responded to my question, I immediately felt the most intense pain I'd ever experienced. A bright beam of morning sunlight struck me and judged me unworthy of its embrace. The blood that still covered my exposed skin bubbled, along with the flesh beneath it. The scent of smoke filled my nostrils as I burst aflame.

A small part of me wanted to let the unnatural fire consume my body and eat away whatever I'd become, but the pain was too intense and I was too weak. I screeched and ran back inside, hoping that nobody saw me. Thankfully, the streets were empty, the residents either already at work for the morning shift or sound asleep.

I reentered the apartment and slammed the door behind me before curling myself into a ball and trying my best not to cry out. Tears streamed down my face, although whether from the pain or what I had done to Mark, I wasn't sure. All I knew was that I dared not look toward the bedroom where his body still lay.

Soon, a strange thing happened. The pain began to fade. I risked a look at my charred flesh, the scars that I would rightfully wear - marked as the Judas I now was. I held up my hand and stifled a gasp. Before my eyes, blackened flesh regained its color. Angry blisters started to recess back into my skin, losing all definition until I couldn't even tell they were there. My body was somehow healing itself at an astounding rate.

It was all too much. My sanity began to tear loose from its moorings. Everything in the past several hours had been akin to a nightmare. I needed something...something *normal* to tell me that there was still hope - that this could still be some far-out hallucination.

God help me, but I needed my family.

I grabbed Mark's phone and hesitated for just a moment before putting my finger in the rotary and dialing. It had been so long, and they were going to be so angry, but that was okay. I could deal with their disappointment in me because it was real, tangible...*normal*.

It rang five times on their end. I was about to hang up when I heard it answered at last.

"Hello?" a sleepy voice asked.

"Linda?"

"Yeah. Who is this? Do you know what time it is?"

"It's Lucinda. Listen, I know it's been...

"*Lucinda*? You've got a lot of nerve calling. You've put Mother through hell, wondering if you were alive or dead."

"What? I thought Uncle Colin told Dad I was okay."

"What are you blabbering about? We haven't seen Colin in over a year, since right before you left.

Considering our father was given the pink slip eight months ago when his department closed, I doubt we'll be seeing him again."

"That can't be right. He said..."

"Are you drunk?"

"Huh?"

"Stoned, maybe? Because if you're calling for money, I'll just tell you right now there isn't any. I had to move back in to help with the bills, all while you...where are you, anyway?"

"I'm in Las Vegas. Listen, Linda, I'm sorry if I..."

"Las Vegas? You fucking bitch! Mom's a mess and Dad's started drinking again and you're off partying like some *whore*."

"It's not like that. Something bad happened. Please, put..."

"No, I don't think so. We have enough problems without you. Just do us a favor and forget this number. Pretend we're dead, because you sure as hell are to us."

"Wait, please!"

My pleading came too late, though. The only reply was the beeping of the disconnected line. I considered calling back, giving my sister a piece of my mind, but realized it would be futile. She was the same old Linda. Some things never changed.

In frustration, I slammed down the receiver - shattering both it and the base. I jumped at the savage display of strength. It was just one more reminder that whatever I was now, it wasn't human.

No! I refused to accept that fate. It had to be wrong. This whole mess had to be some horrible mistake and I'd prove it. I had a life. I just needed to embrace it...live it as if normal. If that happened, maybe I'd wake up tomorrow to find that the whole affair had been nothing but a dream. I wouldn't give in to the nightmare. It had no power over me.

I opened up Mark's closet and found what I needed. Donning the raincoat, and throwing a bath towel over my head, I once more made for the door.

I busied myself for the remainder of the day. After arriving home, I took a shower, closing my eyes so as not to see what washed down the drain. When I was finished, I dared a peek into the mirror and smiled at what I saw. I wasn't some disfigured burn victim. My old self stared back. Maybe whatever was in those drugs was finally wearing off, but I needed to be sure.

Ignoring the strange weariness that I felt, I dove into the most mundane thing I could think of: house-work. After closing the blinds and taking the phone off the hook, I cleaned my small studio apartment, washed the dishes, folded laundry, and rearranged my meager possessions...with the exception of a picture of my family. I wasn't sure the phone call with my bitch of a sister hadn't been imagined, but nevertheless felt no need to feel her accusing eyes upon me. That particular item went straight into the bottom drawer of my dresser.

I worked up a good sweat, or at least I should have. Though my eyes wanted to close, demanding sleep, my body seemed to have endless energy. By the time I was finished, my heart should have been pounding, but instead I felt nothing in my chest - not even the need to breathe harder. Maybe all those nights of dancing were finally paying off. Yeah, that had to be it.

Technically, I was supposed to be at the club by four, but I tarried a bit longer in my tasks than usual. There wasn't any reason for it - or so I told myself - I just wanted to make sure my place was tidy.

Finally, I risked a quick glance out my lone window. Oh dear, it seemed I'd worked until the sun had started to set. Marlene might be mad, but I could just tell her I'd felt ill during the day and had slept late. She'd understand.

Rushing out the door and into the rapidly approaching night, I felt good - like my life was mine once again.

I'd go to the club, dance for a few hours, then pop by Mark's. Maybe I'd even tell him about the crazy dreams of the past day. Then we'd have a good laugh as I described how I'd become a crazed animal and *killed* him.

"Here's to a normal night," I said, smiling as I locked the door behind me.

22

CRACK*

*Mark's fist impacted with my jaw again and I spat more blood. Marlene's goons had dragged Christy and me upstairs. There, she'd compelled me to plant my ass again. Apparently Marlene's connections with the wizards in town were better than I'd have thought possible. Christy was bound to a chair with old-fashioned manacles that were aged and rusty, but not so much that the symbols carved into them weren't visible. They weren't entirely dissimilar to the scrying wards I had painted on the walls of one of my coven's safe houses. Considering the surprised look on Christy's face when she saw them, it was a safe bet to assume they were designed to keep a witch like her from causing any trouble.

I wasn't sure what they had planned for her, but they seemed to have something in mind for me, which, at the very least, involved my former boyfriend beating me to a pulp. What can I say? I apparently have quite the talent for getting into abusive relationships.

"You killed me, Lucinda. Killed me like a dog and just left me there."

"I didn't know," I said, once my mouth wasn't full of fist.

"How could you not?!" he screamed as he back-handed me.

Ow!

"Well, I mean...I knew I killed you," I replied defiantly. "I just didn't realize you had turned."

"Is that supposed to make me feel better? Do you know what I did when I woke up? I killed every single person in my building." He grasped my chin, forcing me to look up at him. "Some of them were my friends."

"I'm sorry."

"Are you? I highly doubt that."

Mark was wrong on that count. He wasn't the only one who'd lost friends that day.

1979

"Jeez, Lu, you're late. Marlene's gonna pitch a nicotine fit," Tina, a slender brunette who danced under the stage name Bambi, said. Her tone was stern, but there wasn't any real animosity behind it. We'd always gotten along well. Heck, I had even babysat her son on a few occasions.

"Nah, I heard she switched to menthols," joked

Minnie, a young dancer who'd been hired around the same time as I had and who loved to share the latest gossip amongst the club.

I gave a small smile, walked over to the mirror, and began applying my makeup. This was my normal, and I was happy to have it.

"I know why she's really late," said a voice from the door. It was Betty. She was already wearing her tassels and not much else. She flipped her flaming red hair over one shoulder with a shake as she walked into the dressing room. "Seems like little Lucinda here has finally gotten with the program."

"Don't be silly," I said, concentrating on my eyeliner.

"What do you mean, program?" Minnie asked. She was a nice girl, but a little dense at times.

"No way. Not Lu," Tina said. "She's not one to turn tricks."

"Oh...Oh!" Minnie cried, catching on. "Really? What happened? Spill!"

"Nothing happened," I replied. "I just had a rough night."

"Oh?" Betty sauntered up. Her eyes mocked me in the mirror. "Then who was that guy you left with last night? He didn't look like your dump of a boyfriend."

"Leave Mark out of this," I warned as my temper rose. That was surprising. Normally, I was above letting a little verbal sparring rattle me. It wasn't like me to have a short fuse.

"So where'd you do it?" she asked. "His room? A friend's place..."

"Yeah, Lu," Minnie joined in the teasing. "Come on, tell us."

"Let's just drop it." The eyelash curler snapped in my grasp. "Goddamnit!"

"Sounds like someone is fibbing," Betty mocked, leaning over my shoulder. Her breasts poked me in the back, further violating my personal space.

"Leave her alone, Bets," Tina scolded. "She said she had a hard night."

"Oh, I bet she did." She leaned close to my ear. Her breath puffed against my neck. I could smell the perfume she wore, could hear the beating of her heart. Oh no! I closed my eyes and willed it to go away. "How *hard* was your night, little Lucinda?"

"Please," I begged. Something sharp pressed against my tongue...make that *two* sharp somethings.

"You're not better than any of us," Betty said. "And you're certainly not too good to make a few extra bucks on the side. So tell us, how was he? He was pretty muscular. I bet he liked the rough stuff."

She grabbed hold of my shoulders and spun me to face her. The scent of her perfume gave way to the smell of the blood that flowed through her veins. That pushed me over the edge. The semblance of normal that I'd been grasping slipped through my fingers. I opened my eyes and grinned.

"What the fuck?" she gasped, no doubt seeing black, soulless pits staring back at her.

Before I knew what I was doing, I backhanded her and sent her flying across the room. Betty and I hadn't hit it off, but I'd never wished her ill before. Now, though, I found myself oddly enjoying what was to come. She and her red hair that men would go crazy for. The fucking whore was all too willing to give them whatever they wanted for a price.

I paused, wondering where these thoughts had come from. It was like all the repressed anger I kept locked up inside of me was loose. The girls in the room had once been my colleagues, and some of them my friends, but now they seemed so small, so insignificant. Playthings for my amusement, nothing more.

"Oh my God!" Minnie shrieked. "What's wrong with you, Lu?" She stepped up and slapped me across the face.

She never was that bright. All Minnie had going for her was her body. Where would she be in a few years when age caught up to her? She had no future to speak of. This place would use her up and then spit her out.

In some ways, I was doing her a favor.

I reached out and grabbed the sides of her head, violently twisting it with the unnatural strength that was now at my disposal. Her vertebrae snapped like matchsticks. I held her up for a moment longer, watching the light die from her eyes. It was a fascinating thing to see. How had I never considered doing this before? It suddenly seemed like the most natural thing in the world.

She dropped bonelessly to the floor. The sound of her heartbeat faded to nothing in my now overly-sensitive ears. Such a fragile thing was life. All too easy to snuff out, and far too tempting to resist doing so.

Betty was slumped against the wall, stunned from my blow. She wasn't going anywhere. That left Tina.

She was a smart girl, far brighter than Minnie had been. Seeing what I'd become, she didn't hesitate for more than second. Letting out a screech of horror, she turned and raced to the dressing room door.

I was on her before she could open it more than an inch. Her screams would probably attract security, but that was okay with me. The party was just getting started, and I was anxious to greet some more guests.

I shoved her forward, slamming the door shut and breaking her nose against it. A small voice inside of me cried out. Tina was a good person, a friend. She had a six-year-old boy, Brock, who would draw the sweetest pictures at school - pictures that she always hung up on her refrigerator.

I laughed. As if such petty mercy meant anything to me. I wrapped an arm around Tina's neck, cutting off her air. I began to drag her back toward where Betty still lay. Her nails scraped against my flesh in a futile attempt to break free. The pain of her finger-nails digging into my arm was strangely enjoyable.

Little Lucinda had been my nickname amongst them, a playful jest upon my size. That girl was gone now. In her place stood a creature of stature. Try as Tina might, I didn't loosen my grip for even a moment. Within a minute, her struggles weakened. I found myself somewhat disappointed it was ending so soon. I was almost tempted to let up just enough for her to take a gulp of air...almost.

Her life force slipped away and I dropped the useless bag of meat left behind. I smiled and licked my lips. Only Betty remained, and sadly for her, my little display had worked up a bit of a thirst in me.

I'd given her enough time to recover, though. She blinked and her eyes began to clear. She kicked out her left leg and hit me in the shin. It was a pathetic blow - I barely felt it - but it ruined my balance and I went down to one knee. Nice! I'd underestimated her. She was a bit of a survivor after all.

She began scrambling backward, away from me. She'd picked the wrong direction, though. Rather than head toward the door, all that was behind her was wall. I grabbed her foot before she could escape my reach and dragged her toward me.

A flash of wicked inspiration hit me. I grabbed at the cheap skirt she wore and ripped it away, revealing her g-string - the one that, on any other night, would be full of bills in just a few hours hence. A lucky customer might even find himself buying a chance to remove it, if he produced enough money.

I shoved her legs apart and she let out a wail.

"What's the matter, Betty?" I asked, innocently. "I thought this was right up your alley." I opened my mouth and bit down on her inner thigh. My nose guided me to the blood - a major artery. I tore open her flesh and began to devour her very essence. She fought back, hands tearing at my hair and beating down on my neck and shoulders. It just made me want her more. Oh God, I had never felt so turned on before.

She continued to shriek as I drank and became drenched in the torrent that flowed from her. I reached up and grabbed one arm that was entangled in my hair, playfully snapping her wrist in the process.

I lost myself in her. Her fear and struggles added to the incredible taste. It was as if a fine chef had seasoned her, turning what would have otherwise been a gourmet meal into a feast fit for a queen.

I became dimly aware that the blood slackened along with her will to fight. That was okay. I would allow her the peace that death...

Rough hands grabbed my arms and dragged me away, interrupting my intimate moment. I was pulled to my feet and spun around. The granite-like visage of Colt, our chief bouncer, met mine. I snarled and threw a punch, wondering how it would feel to rip through his muscular chest and tear his still-beating heart out.

Imagine my surprise when he caught my fist in his meaty hand. I tried to pull away, but his grip was like a vise. It was impossible. I'd torn through people - *my friends* - like they'd been made of tissue paper. There was no way he should have been able to...

That's when his eyes turned black and he flashed fangs of his own. There were more like me? He was one, too? Had Jeff infected others at the club?

Sadly, answers weren't forthcoming. The next thing I knew, Colt's fist slammed into my jaw, sending me spiraling down into the comforting darkness of oblivion.

23

CRACK*

*Mark clocked me in the face again. It was starting to get tiresome. Compulsion would be useless against him. Sure, I'd turned him, which would give me an edge, but our closeness in age would mean he'd be able to fight back and quite possibly shake me off.

I decided to try talking instead. If I could get him to start yammering, at least I wouldn't be force-fed knuckle sandwiches. "Are we gonna keep up this foreplay for much longer, or are we going to finally get to the point?"

"I'd heard that you'd grown up. That the little girl I loved was now a big bad woman calling the shots. Not calling anything now, though, are you?"

Oh he didn't just say the L word, did he? I really hoped that all this bullshit wasn't because he was still smitten with me. That would kind of suck for him.

He'd been a nice guy, but I'd gotten over him a long time ago.

At least, I was fairly sure I had.

"Wait," said Christy. "*This* is the guy you were telling me about? He's the man you were dating back when you were still..."

"Say the word 'human', witch," Mark replied, his claws extending, "and I will cut your unborn child right out of your stomach."

Christy's gaze carried with it a look of pure unadulterated murder, but she immediately clammed up. I could see why. He had meant every word. I wasn't the only one who'd grown up.

"What happened to you?" I asked, truthfully wanting to know.

"What happened to me? What happened to *me*?! After you murdered me, I had nothing. I had no idea who I was. *What* I was. Unlike you, I didn't have the fancy clothes or high-rise apartments. I didn't live the high life and sure as shit didn't have fate drop our legendary savior right into my lap. You've been given everything. I, on the other hand, went underground, surviving off of rats and any derelicts I could catch. I lived that way for years. During those dark times, I used to pray that you'd come back. That you'd explain what had happened and offer me a way for salvation. *Together,* we could have done it." His voice started to crack. If he began crying, I was seriously going to consider asking that he stake me and get it over with. I really wasn't in the mood for a sob story.

"Let me guess. Eventually, Marlene found you."

"Yes. Where you failed me, she was my angel. She

pulled me from the pits of despair and offered me a new option. She took me under her wing and showed me that not only could I live again, but I could be better than I ever was before. I could have all those things you had, and more."

"So where does Kara come into this?" Christy asked, unable to keep her mouth shut.

It was a mistake. Mark backhanded her without his gaze leaving me. Her head rocked back and she went limp. I could hear her taking ragged breaths, which was good, but she was out for the count.

"Yeah," I added, making sure his attention remained on me lest he decide to follow up on his earlier threat. "If, as you said, you had it all, then why bother with her? Why come all the way across the country to pick up some ditzy teenager from Jersey?"

"It's simple," Marlene's voice replied from the second floor landing onto which she'd just stepped. "It's because you fucked us all."

1979

"*WAKE UP!!*"

Instantly, my eyes popped open. One moment I was in unthinking darkness, and the next I was wide awake. I blinked a few times and looked around. Large hands grasped me on either side, holding me upright. Colt's I guessed. We stood in the main room, next to the stage. Marlene was there, glaring at me.

I looked past her and my breath caught in my throat. Behind her was Uncle Colin, but that wasn't who'd caught my attention. Jeff stood there, too. The smug look upon his face told me he was well aware of what he'd done.

The urges that had taken hold of me in the dressing room had subsided, which meant I had no desire to see him take any other victims.

"Watch out, Uncle Colin! He's a..."

"A what?" Marlene's eyes turned momentarily black. She was one of them?! Oh God! "Do you even have the faintest clue of who you are or what you've done? *NOW SIT DOWN AND BEHAVE!!*"

All at once, my mind became all cloudy. I opened my mouth to cry out, but had no voice. My throat had sealed itself shut. It was as if I was plunged into a dream. Marlene's words were...*overpowering*, the word of God himself. I couldn't resist and had no desire to.

"That's a good girl." She reached out and gently caressed my cheek, tracing a line down my jaw and neck with one finger. Her face shone with disappointment. "Such a waste."

I became vaguely aware of Colt's hands letting go of me. Rather than run, which was what I should have done, I calmly walked over to the bar and sat on a stool.

Marlene turned around. "Now, Colin, let's have a little chat."

Colin? *Uncle* Colin? Oh no! I found the strength to fight and the mist cleared from my head a bit. Jeff, Colt, and now Marlene? All of them were those...*things*. I wouldn't let them take Uncle Colin, too.

"Run!" I shouted, finding my voice again. "They're monsters! Save yourself!"

Marlene turned back to me, a look of both disgust and pity upon her face. She opened her mouth, perhaps to command me again, but Uncle Colin put a hand upon her shoulder. What was he doing? Didn't he realize the danger?

"I'll handle this, Marlene, my dear," he said smoothly. Something in his voice had changed. Gone was the paternal tone he'd used so often with me. In its place, arrogance had seeped in. "After all, I do feel this is partially my fault."

"Partially?" she growled. Her eyes turned black once more.

"Now now, let's not forget we're civilized beings." He strolled over to me with a casual gait, as if he had all the time in the world. He stopped short and looked down upon me, his expression unreadable.

Feeling tears well up in my eyes, I opened my arms and reached out to him, seeking what little comfort I could. Neither of us were going to get out of this alive, but knowing that someone I trusted was here made it seem...

He stepped back before I could touch him, leaving me grasping nothing but air. I looked up at him confused as a short bark of laughter echoed from Jeff.

"Now now, none of that, Lucinda," Uncle Colin said. "This is an imported shirt. Italian silk. Blood simply won't come out of it. I'm sure you can understand."

"I don't understand any of this!"

"That's regrettable," he replied. "You had such potential once upon a time. Now...well, look how far you've fallen." He quickly inclined his head back toward Marlene. "No offense intended to your business, oh gracious host."

She opened her mouth as if to respond, but Uncle Colin turned to face me again before she could say anything. "I suppose it's not entirely your fault. For all of his technical foresight, your father was always mired in the past as far as his wife and daughters were concerned. I should have supposed he'd have this effect on you. If he hadn't been useful otherwise, I'd have thought to have killed him rather than let him spoil you with his petty ideals." He smiled, revealing his fangs.

Something inside of me died at the sight. I finally understood that the nightmare was real and I wouldn't wake up from it ever again.

"How long?" I whimpered. "Did he..." I raised a hand and pointed it toward Jeff, who continued to stand there, smirking as if he found the whole thing uproariously funny.

Uncle Colin laughed as if he sensed the same humor Jeff was feeling. "Oh no, you misunderstand, my darling. I've walked in darkness since long before you met me...*far* longer, in fact."

His words hit my gut like a pair of brass knuckles. "So all this time..."

"Doing business with humans is a necessity of my post, I'm afraid. As for you, well, I'd be doing my kind a disservice if I didn't keep my eyes out for those with promise. I had hoped that one day I might recruit you for my team. I see now that was mere folly. Still, you have proven to be of amusement to my associate here. At the very least, I dare say you've filled out nicely. I suppose that counts for something. That could..."

"You fuck!" I screamed. "You motherfucking son of a bitch! I trusted you." I stood and took a step forward. "All this time, I trusted you!" With that, I lost it. My own teeth extended and the red rage from earlier descended upon me. I lunged at Colin, intent on rending the asshole to shreds.

Again, nothing but air met my advance. He side-stepped me neatly, as if I'd been moving in slow motion. I turned, ready to try again, but the opportunity had been squandered.

"Enough of this," Marlene spat. "*SIT DOWN AND BE QUIET!!*"

Her words echoed in my mind and blotted out all other thought. Unable to resist, I walked back over to my stool and sat. I tried to open my mouth to cry out in protest, but found even that was denied me. I sat there, mute, unable to do anything but watch and listen.

"Much better. I'm sure that was all touching to you, Lucinda, but your superiors have matters to discuss now. More importantly," she said, addressing Colin, "the grievances I have against your little pissant here for turning one of my girls without permission."

"Sorry about that, Marl." Jeff sauntered up to her. "It's all cool, though. What's one whore? She's noth...URK!"

Like a flash, Marlene's hand shot out and grabbed

him by the throat. I watched, amazed, as she lifted him from the floor. He was twice her size, but she treated him as if he was no better than a ragdoll.

"You listen to me, you spoiled little brat. She wasn't yours. Not only did you steal from me, but you've caused considerable collateral damage as well. I have two other girls dead and a third who's probably turning as we speak."

"They...can...be..."

"That isn't the point! I'm going to have to close my club tonight because of your greedy stupidity. I haven't had to do so in nearly fifty years because others have been smart enough to play by the rules. You've broken those rules. Now I'm going to..."

"Marlene," Colin said with a bored tone, "I'm sure more violence is unnecessary. Jeffrey here was simply a tad over-enthusiastic, that's all. He's just won over leadership of his own coven. In New York City, no less. I'm sure James would be less than pleased if his newest coven master's reign ended before it even began."

"Do you think that means anything to me?" she replied. "In case you haven't noticed, I'm not under Boston's jurisdiction. The fact that you're his toady means less than nothing here."

"Of course not. I never meant to imply such. However, my position does offer a few perks that may be applicable. I am authorized to offer reparations in regrettable times such as these."

Marlene released her grip on Jeff. He dropped to the floor, clutching his throat. I wasn't sure what it told me, other than he wasn't invincible. If that were the case, did that mean none of them were? At the very least, it was something to remember.

"Fine, let's talk."

"Very well. What would you consider fair trade for two of your girls?"

"Two? I counted four."

"Two dead..."

"And two turned, one of whom was my best earner."

I bristled at the comment. No doubt she was referring to Betty, for whom there was no such thing as a line in the sand that enough dollars couldn't erase.

"Well surely you have..."

"No, I don't. All my girls are human. I'm the only queen in this hive and I like it that way. Besides, little Lucinda here has already shown she can't control herself. I don't need her losing her shit when this place is open. It's bad for business."

"As I can surely understand. I suppose, then, that you are planning on disposing of her and the one she sired."

Marlene's gaze turned momentarily toward me, her eyes taking me in from head to toe. Once more, the look on her face read disappointment, although for what, I wasn't sure. "You suppose correctly."

24

"**F**ucked you all? I mean sure, maybe Mark once upon a time, but I'm fairly certain you and I never..."

"*ZIP IT!!*"

Marlene sure did like throwing the compulsions around. She'd once referred to herself as the queen bee and it was clearly a role she lived up to. No dissension allowed in the ranks whatsoever. I could dig that. Considering the bullshit I had been dealing with at home, perhaps it was a policy I needed to adopt.

"You have no idea what you've done - how you've destroyed me and everything I've built. You're the same stupid girl I used to know. No amount of fashion or attitude will ever change that."

I tilted my head confusedly, my eyes looking around. My meaning was hopefully obvious: this place looked fine to me.

She sighed and put her hands on her hips. "*YOU*

MAY SPEAK!! But be warned, girl, any more sass and I'll compel you to bite off your own tongue and swallow it."

Well, that was a novel idea. I'd have to remember it. "Thank you. In case my meaning wasn't clear, I have no idea what the fuck you're talking about."

"This place used to be a Mecca of vampire hedonism. Covens from all over the world would come here to indulge themselves in all I had to offer."

I figuratively bit my tongue at that. All *she* had to offer? That was a good one. Who knew how many girls had nights they could no longer remember because of her? Hell, who knew how many girls never had another night at all thanks to some over-enthusiastic *guests*?

"Did you know that no less than three of the First Coven have visited my lair?" she asked, continuing onward toward what I hoped was a point.

"Can't say that I do."

"But that's all over now. You're the first *tourist* I've seen in two months, but that's not the worst of it. We're being boxed in from all sides, slowly being squeezed, and nobody is doing a goddamned thing to help us. I have faithfully served the First for over two hundred years, yet my pleas for help fall upon deaf ears. Mark and his security team are the only thing standing..."

"Wait, *Mark's* team? I thought Colt ran security."

"Colt's dead," Mark said. "They got him in the tunnels a month and a half ago, right before we sealed them up."

"Congrats on the promotion." Wait, tunnels?

They? Realization hit. The creatures I'd seen in the casino weren't preparing an attack. One was already well underway.

"You've seen them, haven't you?" Marlene asked. "I can tell by the look on your face."

I glanced over at Christy. She was still out cold. There was probably no point in playing dumb - that would, no doubt, lead to horrific torture and other such fun stuff. Most vamps were nothing if not predicable. "What are they?"

"I don't know," she replied. "There are legends, of course. Skinwalkers. Wendigos. The Shoshone seem to have it the closest. Their legends tell of devils that were driven deep into the Earth eons ago. That makes the most sense. That's where it started, the tunnels."

"When?"

"When do you think, child? Right around the time you and your goddamned Freewill were up in Canada, dragging all of us into a war we didn't ask for."

Oh, yeah. That.

"We didn't think anything about that first storm...just some weird lightning. I had men down below at the time, hunting for some refreshments. Three of them didn't come back."

"Got lost, maybe?"

My answer was another slap to the face. I probably deserved that one.

"Each time one of those storms hit, it gets a little worse...they get bolder. Soon, whatever it is that's holding them back is going to snap and they're going to overrun us. You are directly responsible. If anything, I consider it divine retribution that you're here now just as another storm is forming."

"I've always had impeccable timing..."

"You fucked us all up north! But you weren't finished with just that, were you?"

"I wasn't?"

"While we've been suffering losses, you and that asshole friend of yours had to suck up much needed resources to kill the goddamned Icon...resources that were wiped out to the man, and for what? Hell, you couldn't even do that right. From what I've heard, its body went missing."

What the fuck?! That wasn't common knowledge. Hell, it wasn't even *uncommon* knowledge. I glanced sideways at Christy, for the first time thankful she was unconscious. As far as she and nearly all of the rest of the supernatural world were concerned, the Icon was dead and planted six feet under. The only other person who knew the truth was thousands of miles away in the deserts of Mongolia, and I had a feeling she wasn't one to run her mouth off to the likes of Marlene. I mean, it was possible Starlight had figured stuff out...she was my go-to girl these days, but she wouldn't have known the Pandora Coven from a hole in the wall. She was a New York girl through and through. Who else...

"Still haven't figured it out, have you?" Marlene asked. "How is Betty anyway? When you see her, please send my regards."

"Her? *Firebird*?"

"She's been my eyes and ears there for years. You didn't think I'd let two of my girls leave without at least occasionally checking on you. Certainly most of what she had to say was next to useless, but after Jeff died, her information began to get steadily more interesting. She's a good girl. Never forgot her roots, unlike some."

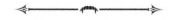

1979

"I'll take her."

"What?"

"I said I'll take her," Jeff repeated, apparently no worse for wear from having Marlene nearly strangle him.

"Oh?" Colin asked, seemingly intrigued.

"Sure. I kinda like her." He walked over to me and ran his hand through my hair. I couldn't even open my mouth to protest. All I could do was mutely shake with rage. "We had a good time, didn't we, Lucinda? I think we can have some more...although that name, it's gonna have to go."

"Are you sure?" Colin asked, as if I was some puppy waiting to be adopted. "She's not quite what I'd hoped she'd be."

"Oh, I don't know. Look at what she did in the other room. She's got potential to be a wolf in sheep's clothing. Greenwich Coven could use someone like that. Not to mention," he added, turning his eyes toward the stage, "I wouldn't mind putting her *other* skills to my personal use."

"Very well," Colin replied smugly. His eyes

regarded me as no more than property to be bartered. "What say you, Marlene?"

I couldn't believe it. He'd been like family to me. Hell, I had loved him like a real uncle and it was all a lie. I silently swore not to forget any of this.

"Fine," Marlene sniffed. "That's one, but it still doesn't solve the problem of..."

"I'll take the redhead, too," Jeff added. "I can make a few openings. Clean out the old regime a bit. I'll admit I'm dying to sample her wares, too." Revulsion filled me. What were we to these people - just pieces of meat? "Two for the price of..."

"Four," Marlene finished, turning to Colin.

"Of course," he replied. "You may name your price. We'll draw up terms later this night."

That seemed to satisfy all the parties in the room, save me, of course. So that was it? Not only was I robbed of my humanity, my normalcy, but now I'd been sold like cattle. Perhaps it was what I deserved. Hadn't I done enough damage? I'd murdered my lover, as well as two of my friends - making an orphan out of a child in the process. To add to my crimes, I'd damned a fourth person to the same Hell as myself.

Colin, perhaps sensing my rage and despair, stepped over and placed a hand on my cheek, mocking the loving gesture that I now knew he was incapable of. I wanted to spit in his face and claw his damned eyes out, but was still under whatever spell Marlene had placed over me.

"Do not fret, my dear. It may seem frightening now, but you have no idea of the world you are about to enter. You've already gotten a glimpse, though.

Strength, speed, power...it's all yours now. As Jeffrey said, you are now a wolf amongst sheep, standing above them in every way. The only beings you answer to now are others of your kind - your elders. We are your parents, your new family, and soon you'll have plenty of brothers and sisters, too. It may be hard to imagine right at this moment, but you may even find your new life to be quite palatable - assuming, of course, you satisfy your new master's needs. But I think you will. You were once a smart girl, Lucinda. I bet she's still hiding somewhere inside of you. If you can find her, you may not only survive, you might be able to thrive. Only time will tell."

25

I was shocked. I hadn't thought Firebird to have either the brains to secretly keep Marlene up to date or the stones to do so, especially during Jeff's reign.

She'd taken to vampirism well. After the initial shock, she was delighted at the prospect of being young and beautiful forever. It didn't matter to her that we were effectively Jeff's property. She was used to doing as she was told, and the perks more than made up for it as far as she was concerned.

Shock at her betrayal gave way to rage. I couldn't have cared less that she'd been blabbing to Marlene while Jeff was busy using us all as his personal playthings. What infuriated me, though, was that she continued doing so after Bill and I took over.

Part of that anger was internal - it meant I had been sloppy, underestimated her. My disdain had blinded me to the fact that she'd been paying attention, probably even rooting through my files when I wasn't around.

If I got out of this, she and I were going to have a long talk that only one of us would be walking out of alive. For now, though, there were other issues to deal with.

"So all of this..."

"Don't get me wrong, doll," Mark interrupted, "I've been wanting for us to have this reunion for years."

Marlene smiled. "I have to say, Lucinda, you should be flattered. You left quite the impression on him. I even had to compel him to stay put for the first few years. I have no problems with a little revenge, but business is business and Colin did make good on his promise to repay me. It would have been sour grapes to go back on a fair deal. But that's all changed now. The scales are once again tipped. I have suffered greatly because of the machinations you and your friend have put into place. Reparations are needed once again."

"We're just cutting out the middleman this time," Mark added.

"Indeed." She took a quick look at the diamond-encrusted watch upon her arm. "Oh my. The time does fly. Mark, be a good lad and start prepping for tonight. Can't keep our customers waiting."

"On it, boss." He turned to leave.

"And remember, Mark," she called after him, "tonight's going to be a special occasion. I think Lucinda will be returning to the stage for one last encore performance."

I rolled my eyes. God, why couldn't people just take care of business when they were presented with the opportunity? Hadn't anyone else here ever watched a James Bond movie? I mean sure, I'd only done so because of Sean Connery, but that didn't mean I hadn't paid attention to the plot.

"I'll look forward to it." He smirked before leaving the three of us alone, no doubt for some *girl talk*.

"I get why you're mad," I said. "I don't doubt half the covens in the country are freaked out right now."

"The hell with them! Do I look like I give a damn what any of them think? All this coven is to them is a good time, a place for them to get their rocks off bleeding out a few whores. That was all fine and dandy. I knew my place in life and was okay with it. But do you think anyone has raised a finger to help us now? I've sent out entreaties to the nearby covens, to the regional seat of power...hell, even to our stronghold in Europe. I've gotten back nothing. They're tossing us to the side, already written off as casualties of war. I don't know if it's some kind of punishment or not. Maybe they're putting two and two together like I am and somehow tracing the blame for this war back to me. After all, if I'd just staked you like I wanted to, none of this would have happened. Well, it's time to correct that little oversight. It's probably too little, too late, but at least when Pandora's Box closes for good I'll take a little solace in it."

"Uh huh. So since I'm doomed and all, mind filling me in on a few details? Like where the fuck does that girl play into all of this, for example? Seems a bit of a stretch."

"As I said earlier, I was surprised too. Thought we might have to try a few times to lure you out here. It's simple, really. We couldn't just outright kidnap you. You have far too many eyeballs turned your way for that. Fortunately, I had an ally in a key strategic place. I told Betty..."

"Firebird, by the way. That's what she goes by these days."

"Jeffrey's stupid rule?"

"That's what I always said."

"Whatever she cares to be called, I'd ordered her to take stock of your personal situation. She conducted a little reconnaissance work on those outside of the coven, anyone you were close to. Imagine my surprise when it turned out you had been spending a great deal of time with the Freewill's human friends."

Great! I had no idea my extracurricular jaunts with Bill's nerd herd were being watched. I'd really need to reconsider my social calendar once this was all over with.

"Imagine my greater surprise when I learned that you've been canoodling with one of them."

Oh shit. She knew about Ed, too?

"Slumming it much, Lucinda?"

"What? I'm young and single. I play the field."

"Playing with your food? I had thought better of you. Regardless, he was my first choice to go after, but I've been hearing some disturbing news regarding his...*condition*."

"Leave him alone. He's been through enough."

"I couldn't care less about that. What he's been through is nothing compared to what shall come to pass. Nevertheless, I agreed with Mark's suggestion to expand our search parameters a little...and that's when we discovered that the other human, the one mated to this witch, had a sister who was nearly of age."

"So that way if I didn't take the bait, you'd at least get a new piece of tail to exploit."

She smiled. "Dire straits or not, business must go on. I plan to run this place as always until such time as this city burns around me."

"What happens then?"

"Who knows? It might not even matter much. This is only the first wave. Creatures older than even the First can imagine are stirring in the shadows. What you've started is going to tear this world asunder."

"So you'll go down with the ship, at least smug in the satisfaction that you got to take me with you?"

"I like to think of it more as justice...karma, certainly." A thoughtful look crossed over her face for a moment. She put one hand on my shoulder. "Even so, your last few hours need not be entirely unpleasant. I am not completely without mercy."

She lifted a leg and straddled me in the chair. I had to admit that was unexpected.

"What are you doing?"

"Ah Lucinda, so pretty and petite. I'd almost forgotten that you wouldn't remember those nights from all those years ago."

What?! "No, but I always assumed it was because you let visiting vamps use me as a chew toy."

"Guilty as charged," she purred, leaning in closer.

Torture I could handle, but this was getting a little weird. I'd always strictly preferred sausage on my pizza, if you get my drift. Sure, I'd experimented a bit...

"The clients got what they paid for. But not all the time. There were a few nights when I indulged myself. A perk of management, if you will."

Guess I'd experimented more than even I was aware of.

"Listen, Marlene, I'm flattered...really, I am. But I'm afraid the mood is kind of off on account of your plans to humiliate me, probably let Mark rape me, and - oh yeah - *kill me* when this is all over. Don't take any offense. Those things tend to just turn me off a little."

"Have it your way, child. ***SIT THERE, SHUT UP, AND ENJOY THIS!!***"

Ooh, nice on that last one. You didn't see that often in a compulsion. I could see how that could be a form of torture in itself. Imagine disemboweling someone slowly, yet ordering them to have an orgasm at the same time. It was pretty fucking diabolical. I'd have to remember that - might come in handy someday.

Thunder rumbled outside. Marlene stiffened for just a moment as she listened.

"How fitting," she said, then pressed her mouth against mine, her tongue darting in and out. Her hands reached up and grasped my shoulders, digging into them ever so slightly with her claws.

I let out a little moan of pleasure. I *was* going to enjoy this, but not for the reasons she assumed.

It was time to stop the play-acting and end this little game.

I brought the open palm of my hand up and slammed it into the side of her head, most likely shattering her eardrum. She fell to the side with a cry, stunned. As powerful as she was, she hadn't been expecting me to fight back.

There was no reason she should have. She'd been smart. She'd had an ally in a strategic location, known my moves in advance, and compelled me to stay in my spot.

What she hadn't counted on, though, was that I also had allies in strategic locations. And mine were a little bit better connected than hers.

26

1995

"Sally, get your ass in here!"

Oh, Jesus Christ! What did King Shit want now? Couldn't have a moment's peace when that asshole was around.

"Hey, baby, do you have to go?"

"Sorry, the boss is calling." I stood up from the couch and smoothed my dress. The loft was pretty empty tonight. Aside from whatever fuckery was going on in the back room, it was just me, Starlight, and my date. The rest of the coven was either off hunting or doing something else that I probably didn't give a shit about.

Ross, or maybe it was Robert - I couldn't be bothered to remember - stood and put his arms around me. "Come back soon?"

"Sorry, love, but I think this party is over."

"Yeah, but..."

CRACK

Ah, the sound of a broken spine always made me

feel better. I dropped him to the floor and stepped over him.

"Oh, and just for the record," I said, turning back to his corpse, "my eyes are up here, asshole."

"Seems like a waste of a good meal," Starlight said playfully, stepping from the kitchen.

"Feel free. He's still warm."

"Sally!"

"Coming, *master*."

I couldn't wait to see what he wanted now. It was usually related to one of two things: sex or him just being too fucking lazy to do something himself. I wasn't sure which I was beginning to dislike more.

No, actually that was an easy one. He'd been having me translate a lot of letters from Boston as of late. A roll in the sheets was far more preferable to the crash course in ancient Latin I'd had to give myself. There wasn't a whole lot out there on it. I'd even tried checking on that new website...Yahoo! or whatever it was called. Waste of time. On the upside, at least I'd learned a few interesting tidbits...which I guess might help me one day if ever there was an undead equivalent of Jeopardy.

I pushed open the door to the bedroom. As expected, Jeff was lounged naked on the bed. Firebird was there, too, in her natural state...head buried in his lap. Judging by the empty baggies lying about, both were completely fucked up on coke. What a surprise. Jeff hadn't met a recreational drug he didn't like.

Judging by the scene before me, I was about to be *asked* to join them. Guess I'd be needing a second shower today.

"Yes, Night Razor? You summoned?"

"Damn straight I did. I got a job for you."

"Looks like Firebird is already taking care of that."

Had he been in his right mind, he'd probably have been pissed. Jeff didn't like anyone talking back to him, even in jest. Just last week, Rage Vector had cracked a joke that Jeff hadn't liked and gotten his head put through a cinderblock wall for his troubles. It'd been fun to watch, and the truth was the dick-head deserved it, but it served as a good reminder to the rest of us.

Fortunately, Jeff was utterly stoned out of his mind at the moment. He laughed like a jackass at my little joke.

Firebird, for her part, just raised her head enough to glare daggers at me, but I couldn't have cared less about that. Despite our shared history, there was no real love lost between us. We'd stuck together those first few months, each using the other as a sort of life-line to a simpler time. That didn't last long. As we each grew to accept our fate and our new existence, we rapidly grew apart to the point where familiarity definitely bred contempt.

"Heh, good one," Jeff snorted, getting himself under control. "Ozymandias just got into town."

It took me a moment to pull up the name. As a customary show of respect, it was expected for outsiders to conform to a coven's traditions. Unfortunately, one of Jeff's was a stupid edict for us to cast off our old names and take new ones - mostly of his choosing. I'd been saddled with the brilliant moniker Sally Sunset. Yeah, not one of his better choices. Betty had at least gotten Firebird, which, while not original, wasn't overly humiliating. With regards to visitors, Jeff tended to pick names arbitrarily in the moment...the expectation being that everyone else should remember it.

"The Prefect from Boston?"

"One and the same, babe."

That was a bit of a big deal. From what I understood, he had over a dozen covens under his personal command. Rumor had it he was old, making even Jeff look like a child in comparison. It was said he personally knew members of the Draculas, our semi-mystical leadership - ancient creatures who none of us, Jeff included, had ever met. Whatever the case, he was powerful. Even Jeff was afraid of him, although he'd never admit it.

None of that bothered me, though, as much as what it possibly meant.

"Is Colin here, too?" I asked through gritted teeth. Jeff raised an eyebrow. "I meant, is *Armani* in town as well?" I held back a snicker at that. It'd been the best Jeff had come up with at the time...obviously based on Colin's penchant for wearing expensive suits to cover what a slimeball of a shit he was.

"Nope. Ozymandias is here alone. Wants to meet with me tomorrow to discuss some new bullshit restrictions."

"Okay, so what do you need from me?"

"As I just said, that's tomorrow. Tonight, I need someone to go and entertain our guest."

"Entertain?"

"Yeah, show him a good time. Give him whatever he desires. Fulfill every sick fucking fantasy he has."

Oh shit. Jeff was known for sending out sacrificial lambs if the visitor ranked high enough. I'd been lucky enough to avoid that up til now. Thankfully, unlike the rest of this bunch, I had a brain in my fucking head. I'd gotten tons of crap work dumped on me instead, resulting in me being little more than an undead secretary most days, but at least it kept me from being doled out like a whore.

"Firebird usually handles the visiting dignitaries," I pointed out truthfully, if not tactfully. Hell, most of the time she didn't even need to be compelled to do so. She knew her place in the world and was happy with it. Me, not so much.

"Firebird is otherwise occupied," he replied, his tone growing cold.

"What about Starlight?" I hated to throw her under the bus. She was probably the only member of the coven I actually liked. Still, there's that old saying about *better you than me.*

I was pushing my luck with Jeff and knew it. Stoned or not, he was like a spoiled child. The second he didn't get his way, a tantrum was incoming. Considering his power, that was never a good thing.

"*SHOW OZYMANDIAS A GOOD TIME!! DO WHATEVER HE DESIRES!!*"

His voice whipped through my body and erased my own free will. Hah, that was a good one. Vampires actually had a sort of boogeyman of legend called, ironically enough, a Freewill. I'd first heard it through coven gossip, but had learned a bit more through the correspondence Jeff had me translating - something about a prophecy and the end of the world. Real superstitious bullshit. It was nothing to take seriously, albeit I found myself wishing for the power for which they were named - the ability to resist compulsion. Sadly, it was not to be.

"Now get the fuck out of here."

Jeff didn't need to add that last part. Even as he spoke, my body turned and headed toward the door. All I could do was grit my teeth and hope this Ozymandias wasn't the animal his reputation suggested.

I arrived at the twenty-ninth floor of the Carlyle and headed toward the high-priced suites that Boston kept on reserve. One upside to my time as a vampire was learning that poverty wasn't going to be an issue. My coven was well-to-do and that was just the tip of the iceberg. Rumor was the vampire nation was awash with money - old money. The current accommodations seemed to reinforce this notion.

I dreaded what would come next. The front desk told me the room was occupied by one James Ozy, no doubt his play on Jeff's nickname. The second he opened the door, I knew that the compulsion would take over again. Who knew how much blood would paint the walls of his room before the sun rose in the morning...and how much of it would be mine?

"One moment, please," came a deceptively pleasant voice from inside.

A few seconds later, the door opened. The room's occupant was quite striking: short brown hair, hazel eyes, and a strong chin. He was a few inches shorter than Jeff and not quite as muscular, but still solidly built. He looked me in the eye and smiled pleasantly.

"Are you Ozymandias?" A lump rose in my throat. If what I'd heard was true, here stood a guy who predated this country.

He sighed. "I suppose I am, at least when in this city. Please do come in."

"Thanks. I'm Sally, from Village Coven."

"It is a pleasure to make your acquaintance, Ms. Sally." He held out a hand.

I reached out and took it, not sure what to expect, but all he did was give it a gentle shake.

Soft sounds drifted out from the interior and diverted my attention. Cartoonish voices and the occasional outlandish explosion could be heard coming from the bedroom. "Am I interrupting something?"

He raised a bemused eyebrow. "Oh, not at all. That's just the television - a bit of a guilty pleasure, if you will. I occasionally use the downtime that coven visits afford as an excuse to catch up on my pop culture."

I almost grinned despite myself, then quickly covered it up as I remembered who this was.

"In any matter, I assume Jeff...sorry, *Night Razor*. I apologize for my momentary lack of proper protocol."

"Oh...no problem," I replied, amazed to hear that

last sentence. If there was one thing Jeff never did, it was say he was sorry for anything.

"As I was saying, I assume Night Razor sent you to keep me out of trouble for the evening."

"Something like that," I muttered, feeling my eyes lose focus. The edges of the compulsion began to take hold again.

"Excellent. Then what shall we do to kill the time? Pardon the pun."

Almost immediately, my tongue was not my own. "I am here to fulfill whatever you desire."

Ozymandias frowned. "Come again?"

"I am here to fulfill whatever you desire," I repeated, internally screaming out a cry of rage.

He let out another sigh and looked me straight in the eye. "I do so hate when coven leaders send their representatives out with such painfully blatant compulsions. No offense meant to your master, but I dare say Night Razor is one of the worst offenders." He placed his hands on my shoulders. Inwardly I tensed, certain that whatever happened next wouldn't be pleasant. "I apologize in advance if this hurts. *YOU ARE RELEASED FROM YOUR ORDERS!!*"

I staggered in his arms, but he held me up. My god, the power behind his voice - it made Jeff's commands seem like a whisper in comparison. How old was this guy?

"What the fuck?" I gasped, realizing a moment too late what had just escaped my lips.

"A crude, but apt question," he replied, a grin once more covering his face. "Let's test it, shall we?

Are you here to fulfill my deepest and most disturbing desires?"

I opened my mouth, sure Jeff's commands would come pouring out, but found that they weren't there. I squealed with delight at the realization. "Don't take offense to this, but not really."

"Excellent!" he replied, dropping his hands from my shoulders.

"What did you do?"

"I overrode Night Razor's commands."

"You can do that?"

"Oh yes, my dear. Compulsion is considerably more complicated than just giving orders and having them carried out no matter the cost. There are many subtleties involved...one such being that a vampire of sufficient strength can cancel out or even insulate one from another's compulsion."

"Really? I don't suppose you could insulate me from any more of Jeff's orders."

He frowned at that. "You should refer to him as Night Razor. We are in his domain and I am bound by my station to honor his edicts. As you are his charge, you must do likewise. Alas, in answer to your question, I cannot. It would be a violation of my duties to the First Coven. Please don't take offense. Just know I take my station and responsibilities quite seriously."

"Can't blame a girl for trying."

"No, I cannot at that," he replied with a laugh. "Now, how about we begin again? What sights would you care to show me in your fair city?"

"That was simply marvelous!" James...Ozymandias, I had to remind myself...exclaimed as we walked back to his hotel room.

"You mean you've never had espresso before?"

"Of course. I have been around for a while. Even so, that was a particularly good blend. I shall have to remember that place for future visits. In fact, I might have to start finding excuses to come down here more often."

I found myself genuinely smiling. That a being as old as him could find happiness in something as mundane as coffee was refreshing. A small part of me feared that a general malaise would set in after a time - years, possibly centuries, from now. With nothing of interest left, I might just find myself sitting out on the beach, awaiting one last sunrise. Ozymandias's overall attitude gave me reason to push that particular worry aside.

I had to admit, I was actually having a good time. He had no shortage of stories to tell and they were all surprisingly entertaining. I had previously met a few vampires that were older than Jeff and all of them seemed to suffer from the same affliction: being self-absorbed assholes. To meet someone so old, yet so *alive*, was a breath of fresh air. That he was wickedly good-looking didn't exactly hurt, either.

We stopped at the door and he began digging in his pocket for his room key. "I have to say, Sally, you have been quite the engaging company tonight. It's rare that a coven master sends someone so insightful to meet with me."

"Oh?"

"Quite. For example, Night Razor typically sends another member of Village Coven to entertain me when I'm in town...a charming, if somewhat vacuous, redhead. Sadly, her name escapes me."

I had to bite my tongue to keep from laughing out loud.

"Anyway, we often don't even get past the threshold of my hotel room. Don't get me wrong - I have nothing against physical companionship. It's just that it's nice to be able to sit and talk outside of business with someone whose interests lie beyond the usual staples of vampire life."

"Blood?"

"And self-importance."

"Hah! I understand that one. What can I say? I used to be a history buff...a bit of a bookworm."

"Used to be?"

"My father didn't consider education of paramount importance for a woman."

"Forgive my saying so, but he was a fool. I've walked this Earth for many centuries and in that time I've developed a knack for reading people. One need only speak to you for a few moments to see the bright mind behind those lovely eyes. You could do far worse things than indulge your natural curiosity."

"Really?"

"Yes."

I'd been holding back, mostly listening to Ozymandias talk all evening. The truth was there were a ton of vampire-related questions I wanted to ask him, but I'd been afraid. "Well then, what can you tell me about the war?"

"Which one? Civil, Revolutionary, World..."

"The Feet."

His eyes opened slightly in surprise.

"I've been doing some translating for Night Razor, and I've noticed mentions of it here and there. It's..."

He raised a finger to my lips. "Curiosity is a good thing, but it should be tempered where certain business is concerned. Our hierarchy is quite strict, and some are none too pleased to learn when information leaks."

Uh oh.

"Not myself, mind you," he continued, lowering his hand and smiling. "I would rather see our people armed with as much knowledge as they'd dare wish to burden themselves with. Alas, while my power here may seem significant, I'm little more than a cog in the grand scheme of things."

"Somehow, I don't believe that."

He leaned close and whispered, his breath tickling my neck. "Neither do I." He pulled back and raised his voice to normal levels. "But far be it from me to admit so."

He was such an odd duck. The polar opposite of Jeff. Why couldn't I have been recruited into his coven? He seemed like he had a lot to teach, and not just about the fluctuations of the price of drugs.

"Sadly, much of this is moot," he continued, unlocking his door. Pushing it open, he stepped onto the threshold. "I am of the mindset that even if I were given permission to open our archives, offer free access to all who wished it, the flood of those seeking knowledge would be little more than a trickle."

"Agreed. Not to put too blunt of a name to it, but at the very least I know my coven is full to the brim with fucking idiots."

"I won't join in the disparagement of a coven under my charge," he said, "but I find myself unwilling to disagree as well. Take no offense, but your group as a whole is quite the stark contrast compared to a coven up in Cambridge that I oversee. Albeit I would probably call them the exception rather than the rule...and their overall arrogance does tend to grate."

"Well then, Night Razor would fit right in with them...at least, until he opened his mouth."

"I hope you do not speak that way around your master. It has been my impression that he does not tolerate insolence."

"He doesn't tolerate anything that doesn't involve kissing his ass. He's small minded, self-centered, insecure..."

"Do tell me how you really feel, please."

Realizing I was just chewing Jeff a new asshole in front of the guy who was, in essence, his boss - a vampire who'd known him far longer than he'd known me - I quickly changed my tone. "I'm sorry. That was probably out of line."

"It was, but honest opinion is likewise a refreshing breath of air."

"You...won't tell him I said that, will you?"

He leaned against the doorframe and appeared to consider my words. It'd been stupid of me to get comfortable and let my guard down. I'd seen other coven members, a few of them now *former* members, get caught doing the same thing. They'd been whispering in hushed tones, making jokes, not realizing just how acute Jeff's hearing was.

The bottom line was that he owned us wholly. When he wanted something, we knew to submit. There was no defense we could take if he chose to make an example out of us. A brief shudder passed through me as I realized just how afraid of him I was.

I looked up toward Ozymandias, ready to plead my case, but found him grinning.

"I believe the phrase is, we have a deal. I will keep your somewhat low opinion of Night Razor to myself. In return, though, I will require recompense."

Recom...oh. I had thought Ozymandias different, but at the end of the day he was a guy and here I was, standing in his hotel doorway, wearing a dress that didn't leave much of my figure to the imagination.

"I know," he continued. "I shall require your eyes."

"Huh?"

"Not physically, of course, but I'd like for you to be my inside man...in a manner of speaking. I won't lie. Night Razor concerns me. The Greenwich Village Coven is in a key city of this country. There should be more influence wielded, greater ambition shown. Instead, he runs things like one of those discotheques that used to be all the rage."

"Then why don't..."

"Because it is his prerogative to rule his coven however he sees fit. So long as the overarching integrity of the vampire nation is maintained, that is the edict of the First. I am beholden to it."

Realization hit. "You don't like him anymore than I do."

"The enemy of my enemy and all that...albeit I would like to think perhaps we had more than that in common. Regardless, I would ask that from time to time when I visit, you simply fill me in on any goings-on that might be of concern. I don't expect there to be much, but it will make me feel better knowing I am getting an honest opinion rather than the whitewashing that so many coven masters like to give."

There wasn't really much to consider. I liked this guy, whereas Jeff was a fucking cock. Having a friend in high places wouldn't exactly hurt in the long run, either.

"In return," he added, "while I won't divulge state secrets, I will allow you to indulge in your curiosity for some matters, especially as it appears that your position in the coven puts you in the know anyway." He held out his hand to me. "Do we have a deal?"

I reached out, but hesitated for a moment. "What if he finds out?"

"He won't."

"He could compel me to..."

"No, he won't...at least not when I am finished."

"I thought you said you wouldn't insulate me against his commands."

"I did and I spoke true. You are his charge. To do

so would be the height of impropriety on my part. That being said, as I consider our pact to be a matter above his rank, I see no issue protecting questions regarding it."

I laughed, then grasped his hand in mine and nodded.

"*YOU ARE TO IGNORE ANY AND ALL COMPULSIONS REGARDING THE NATURE OF OUR RELATIONSHIP!!*"

It was both powerful and subtle. Unlike a normal compulsion, which rang through one's head and made their body not their own, this one flowed like a lazy river into my subconscious. I felt something akin to a door being locked, one that Jeff didn't have the key to.

We stood there, holding hands for a moment longer, then Ozymandias said, "The pact is sealed. It has truly been a lovely evening with an even lovelier woman. Sadly, dawn is only about an hour away. You should get back to the safety of your..."

He tried to pull away, but I refused to let go of his hand. "How do you do it?"

"Do it?"

"Stay...the way you are. You're so...different. Don't take this the wrong way, but you're so *human*."

"Take that the wrong way? I consider it a compliment. That is exactly my secret. I try to never forget the man I once was. He wasn't perfect by any means, but he tried. I don't often live up to who I wanted to be, but when I fail, I remember my friends, my family, those who are long gone. As long as I can still see their faces, that man isn't entirely forgotten."

He'd been lucky. I thought back to my family. There were few spots in my memories that weren't tinged with resentment and regret.

"Never forget your humanity, Sally."

I sighed sadly. "I think it's too late for me."

"Nonsense. Believe me - once upon a time, I said the same thing. I was wrong. It's only too late when we let it be. Perhaps you just need to be reminded."

"There isn't anyone left to do that."

"Then perhaps one day you'll meet someone who will. Strange times are on the horizon. The vampire nation has prospered, but our overall existence has been stagnant for centuries. That can only last so long before the tide changes and washes complacency away. Such is the nature of the world."

I waited for him to say more, maybe enlighten me as to what he meant, but he was finished. "Now, I really do mean it. You should hurry if you don't wish to be caught in the sun's morning rays."

Again, he tried to disengage his hand from mine, but once more, I didn't let go.

"I...think I'd like to stay, if you don't mind."

"You don't have to do that. As I said at the start of this wonderful evening, you are free from those orders. You need not fulfill any of my desires."

"I'm not," I replied, inching closer. "I'm fulfilling *mine*."

I stepped into his embrace and pushed the door shut behind us.

27

PRESENT DAY

Had he been in the same situation I found myself in with Marlene, Bill would have paused to deliver what he'd no doubt consider to be a witty line. He seemed to do that a lot, despite the fact that it often ended badly for him. That's what you get when your friends are dorks and your babysitter growing up is the TV.

Too bad for my former employer that I wasn't him. She might have otherwise stood a chance.

I was on top of Marlene before she even hit the floor. Without hesitation, my claws extended and I raked them across her throat, severing her carotid arteries and windpipe in the same swipe. I dug deep, making sure that even her advanced healing wouldn't be able to close the wounds in time. Even the most powerful of vampires would be hard pressed to keep going when drained of their lifeblood. She was...

Ugh!

She was still very much in the fight, backhanding

me off of her like I was a gnat. I flew and slammed into the far wall, shattering the full-sized mirror that hung from it and embedding myself into the wood inlay like some sort of bizarre decoration.

I shook my head, clearing it quickly. Fortunately, I'd been ready for her counterattack, using my arms to absorb the brunt of her power. I felt a trickle of blood from a cut that'd been opened in my cheek and smiled. So she wanted to do this the hard way. That was fine by me. Mark and the others were downstairs. Any thumping they heard going on up here would be assumed to be Marlene having her fun with me. Robbed of her voice, she couldn't cry out, and I didn't intend to give her enough time to psychically compel them to her aid.

Extending my fangs, I grabbed a shard of glass from the broken mirror and launched myself from the wall. Marlene was struggling to get back up, her neck a geyser of blood. I plowed into her just before she could regain her footing. The floor was slick with her fluids, and she wasn't able to brace herself. We went down again with me on top. In my life I'd been a meek little mouse, but in my afterlife I'd discovered the dom inside. Being on top offered far more possibilities.

The glass sliced my palm open, but that was okay - nothing compared to the damage I'd done to her. I slammed the shard home into her chest - too far to the side to hit her heart, but more than enough to puncture a lung and maybe a few other organs.

I was tempted to laugh, but kept my mouth shut instead to avoid swallowing any of the fluids that gushed from her. We struggled in relative silence. I wasn't the Freewill. While Bill could gain strength from the blood of other vampires, Marlene's blood was toxic to me. Too bad.

She continued to fight back, grappling and trying to use her superior power. She almost made it. Just as she was on the verge of overcoming my leverage, I felt her strength falter.

Gradually, I forced her arms back down, noting that the fountain of blood had begun to subside.

The fight was over; she was done. I bent down and put my cheek against hers. Almost lovingly, I whispered, "You took everything from me. Now it's time to return the favor."

I sat up and, claws extended, plunged my hand straight into her chest.

Her eyes glared malevolently up at me for a moment longer. In them, I could see the long years she'd lived and worked here, the despair she'd felt at having her world torn asunder. Oh well - they say karma's a bitch.

They're right.

One moment, she was there. The next, a flare of light sparked and her body collapsed in on itself. I found myself sitting on an empty dress. Her ashes settled upon me and stuck, thanks to the amount of blood covering me. It was almost like being tarred and feathered, if a bit more pleasant.

I stood up, dripping various pieces of her, and

looked toward the stairs. No footsteps sounded. That was good. As I'd suspected, any commotion they heard would be assumed to be their master. To most coven vamps, it was nearly inconceivable to consider the alternative. Marlene, like Jeff, had ruled with an iron fist - a god amongst immortals. After a while, one's charges tend to buy into the hype.

Sadly, we still weren't out of the woods. I could celebrate my victory later. For now, I needed to get my shit in gear.

I walked over to where Christy was still shackled. I bent down and gently slapped her cheek, leaving traces of gore on it. She could always freshen up later.

"Come on. Wake up, sleepy head."

"Ugh..."

"That's it. Time to wakey wakey. Your sister-in-law still needs saving."

"Kara, is that you?"

"Not quite."

Christy's eyes opened. She blinked a few times, and then focused on me. They immediately went wide as she took in the sight. I couldn't blame her. I probably looked like I'd just bathed in Marlene's innards, which wasn't far from the truth.

"I take it you won," she said groggily.

"Yep." I reached down and grasped the shackle that held her right arm down. They'd been designed with mages in mind, not vampires. I tore it from its hinges easily, then started to work on the other.

"How?"

I opened my mouth to reply and found that I

couldn't. The words wouldn't come, but then I'd known that would happen.

"I need a favor, James."

"I already know what you're going to ask," he replied from the other end of the phone line.

"She's not my sire or my master, nor is she under your dominion. This is a personal matter between..."

"You need not explain protocol to me, my dear. I am well aware, just as I am aware of your history with Marlene. I hope you know that you've picked a less than ideal time to ask this."

"I know there may be repercussions. She's old and well connected."

"Perhaps not as well connected as you may think," he replied cryptically. "Even if I agree, you'll still be at a disadvantage. Marlene is far older and stronger than you. Insulated or not, you would stand very little chance."

"Then you wouldn't exactly be tipping the odds in my favor."

"True on that."

"So will you? Please?"

"For the sake of what you've done for the vampire nation, I will."

"Thanks, James, and I promise to never tell another soul about it."

"I know you won't, Sally, but I will have to take necessary precautions nevertheless..."

"I'm just that good, I guess," I said with a grin, before steering the conversation away from me. "How are you doing? Anything broken?"

"I'm gonna need an ice pack and some aspirin, but I think I'll be okay." Christy shook her head again, then a panicked look appeared on her face. "Oh my God, what about..."

"Calm down. How do you feel?"

Once freed, her hands went to her stomach. "I don't care about me! What if..."

"The baby's fine."

"How..."

"I can hear two heartbeats. I think it inherited its father's hard head. Doesn't hurt that you got lucky, too. The guy who decked you in the stomach was just a human."

"Yeah, lucky. Sloppy is more like it."

"That too," I chirped, helping her up. "Can you walk?"

"I think so."

"Good, because we're probably going to need to run. I only took out Marlene. The rest are downstairs."

"Kara?"

"Her, too. Happily compelled in lala land."

"What's the plan now?"

"Get her and get the fuck out of here."

"I could have thought of that."

"Well, then, why didn't you?" I turned and began heading further down the hall. There was a second stairwell that came down behind the main dressing room...or at least, there used to be. It was probably a safer plan than just waltzing down the front steps. Before I could take more than a step, though, Christy caught my arm.

"Don't touch him. He's mine."

"Mark and I..."

"The one who punched me," she clarified.

I nodded. "Be my guest." There was a reason one didn't get between a grizzly bear and her cubs.

We turned a corner and she asked, "So that guy, Kara's boyfriend, is really your ex?"

"Yep, that's Mark. Used to be a nice guy."

"Up close, he and Bill look a lot..."

I stopped and glared at her. There was a thought I *really* didn't need bouncing around in my brain.

"Don't even think of finishing that sentence."

28

T he lights flickered. The storm was right on top of us. It gave me an idea...one that was probably suicidal, but an idea nevertheless.

Marlene had made a mistake in choosing to open tonight. Her dedication to keeping the club going, no matter what, was going to cost...

Oh wait, she was already dead. Well, then it was going to cost the yahoos in her employ. With any luck, they'd be hopping around like good little minions, getting ready to open. The dressing room would be filling up with girls by now. That was good. What was one more blonde and brunette amongst the crowd?

If we were lucky, we'd be able to slip out without more than a minimal exchange of hostilities. They'd have the advantage in numbers, although the truth was I had no idea how many we were up against. Other than Marlene, I'd only seen four other vampires and a handful of human thralls. It was possible she'd been in as dire straits as she claimed...

Oh, screw it! I was just bullshitting myself. The real problem was that a part of me was hoping to avoid facing Mark.

A year or two ago, I wouldn't have batted an eye at the concept. We'd have either been cool by now, fucked for old time's sake, or I'd have killed him - hell, probably any two of those. Now, though, thanks to the glass of Bill-flavored humanity that I'd apparently swallowed at some point along the way, I found myself actually feeling guilty about the poor dickhead. He'd been a good man once, but now he was a monster - all thanks to me.

Still, that was neither here nor there. Time to save the pity party. I could let *little Lucinda* out of my subconscious later on to fret about the past. Right now, we still had a job to do, and I was intent on finishing it. I didn't know Kara for shit, but I wouldn't let her fall down the same rabbit hole I had. Fuck history repeating itself.

Luckily, the back stairs were just as I'd remembered them. Marlene hadn't been too big on the concept of total renovations, which was good news for us. She'd been a creature of habit, changing with the times only so much as needed to be done.

Christy and I came out in the main storage room. The hall to the back door, alarmed and guarded even back during my time here, led off to the right. The dressing area was to the left.

"Where is it?" I quietly asked myself.

"Where's what?"

I idly grabbed a bottle of Hennessey from a shelf and popped the cap as I tried to remember the layout from years past.

"You were looking for *that*?"

"Oh, this?" I took a pull. "No, it's just been a long night. I'm trying to remember where the subbasement entrance is."

Maybe I'd been wrong about Marlene's dislike for renovations. It had been right here - a trapdoor down into the...oh yeah. Hadn't Mark said something about the tunnel entrance being sealed? Well, that could make things difficult. If such were the case, we'd have to fight our way out, and sadly, I'd left my favorite handgun back in New York.

There! I spied a collection of crates stacked in one particular spot. A small groove in the floor peeked out beneath them at the edge of the door. That was it? They'd just stacked shit on top of it? Not exactly a top-notch security system. I mean, a few crates wouldn't...

"Ugh!"

I gave them a shove and got nothing for my efforts. Okay, so they were really heavy crates. What the fuck was in them, solid concrete?

"Why'd they cover it up with those?" Christy asked, moving to stand next to me.

She'd been unconscious when Marlene had explained things. It was probably best to not bring her entirely up to speed, lest she think better of our escape route.

"I don't know...big rats, maybe? They probably had some of the tunnel people sneaking in and stealing the liquor."

"You'd think they'd encourage that behavior."

Actually, they had back in the day. Christy was definitely no slouch in the brains department, which once more made me wonder what the fuck she saw in Tom. "You'd think. Sadly, I don't think Marlene will be forthcoming with answers."

"If we can get down there, can you get us to safety?"

"Probably...I mean, sure."

She glanced at me sideways. "Good enough. Stand back; I can take care of this."

"Okay, you...zap it, or whatever it is you do, and I'll grab Kara."

"Where..."

"In the dressing room. I can smell her."

"Do you need my help?"

"No, I'll be fast. Just do whatever you're going to do quietly."

I sniffed the air again outside the dressing room door. Yeah, the girl was in there, along with a few others, all human. It was interesting, Marlene's obsession with keeping all the girls in her employ human. Odd the traditions some coven masters set forth. Guess she didn't want the competition. Still, it wasn't the stupidest rule I'd ever heard of.

I checked the door. Unlocked, as expected. I likewise didn't worry about running into any of Marlene's goons in there. Men were strictly forbidden backstage except during emergencies.

Like when you killed Tina and Minnie?

Ah, memory lane, gotta fucking love it. But now was not the time for that shit. They were long dead and buried, forgotten by all...save, perhaps, me.

I shook my head. Fuck me! When this was over, I really needed to kick back with a pitcher of Bacardi 151 daiquiris until those memories went back to the graveyard where they belonged.

Enough dilly-dallying! I turned the handle, intent on ushering Kara out of there quickly. With any luck, the girls would think I was just part of a different shift and not bat one false eyelash at me.

I opened the door.

Several pairs of pretty young eyes turned in my direction, and then all hell broke loose as the nearest one, a stacked brunette, let out a shrill shriek.

Oh yeah. Guess I should've remembered I was covered head to toe in Marlene's blood. Christ, it can never be easy, can it?

I popped the screamer in the mouth, pulling my punch at the last second. None of these girls deserved to die. Hell, none of them deserved to be disfigured just because I was dumb enough not to shower off before stepping in. They were all me once upon a time.

Goddamnit, I was doing it again. If this kept up, I would be reduced to tears, bawling my eyes out at my lost youth. Fuck that shit!

I put on my game face, blackened my eyes, and

extended my fangs. If these girls thought I looked like some horror show reject, I might as well put it to use and clear myself a path.

Pandemonium was in full force. The girls ran to the other exit, which was fortunate for me. Anyone racing in to help would have to wade through a sea of panicked thongs and teddies.

Only Kara remained at the mirrors. She stood there in matching bra and panties while calmly applying lipstick. Whatever compulsion they'd planted in her head, it was holding fast. Either she had the willpower of a slow-witted puppy or she hadn't been overly terrified enough to try fighting it to begin with.

Mark!

Marlene was powerful enough to put her under this deep, but if Kara had convinced her stupid self that she was in love with Mark, then he could've done so without raising one iota of a subconscious protest in her mind.

That was also fortuitous for me. I couldn't undo a compulsion by Marlene, but I was older than Mark...even if only by a few hours.

I grabbed her shoulder and spun her to face me.

"*WAKE UP!!*"

Just to be on the safe side, I planted a healthy smack on her face. Not hard enough to hurt, but more than enough to get her attention.

Her hand flew to her cheek and the glaze in her eyes cleared almost instantly. They opened wide as she took in my appearance, looking like I'd stepped from the final scene of *Carrie*.

"Who are you?"

"Hi, I'm Sally and you're coming the fuck with me." I grabbed her wrist and, without further ado, dragged her with me to the back door.

She let out a shriek in protest - what a whiner - but was unable to do anything, save follow me. "Please don't hurt me!"

"Duly noted," I replied, pulling the door shut behind us and snapping the knob off.

"Listen, if its money you want, I can..."

"We can compare credit reports on the second date." I gave her a shove forward into the storage room.

Christy ran out to greet us. "I thought you said to be quiet."

"Those who can't do, teach."

The startled girl turned toward her. Recognition dawned on her face, but not the relief I'd been expecting. "What are you doing here?"

"It's okay, Kara. I'm here to take you back home to your parents. It's going to be all right."

The girl's tone immediately changed to defensive. "It was already all right. I'm not going back home, and I sure as shit didn't need your help, bitch."

I raised a questioning eye to Christy.

"What? I never claimed she liked me."

"Okay, you two skanks need to get the fuck out of here before my boyfriend..."

"Enough of this shit," I snarled. I grabbed Kara once more by the wrist and dragged her with me. "I have news for you, sweetheart. Your boyfriend is dead."

"Dead?! You killed Mark?"

"Yeah," I turned to face her. "About thirty years ago, and if you don't stop fucking around, he's going to return the favor to all of us."

29

Christy had been good to her word. She'd not only somehow moved the crates off the trapdoor, but she'd melted a heavy padlock that had been used to lock it.

It was handy to have a witch around. I briefly considered offering her a job on my payroll before dismissing the idea. There would be time for discussing staff additions later. The sound of someone breaking down the back door of the dressing room reached my ears. They were coming.

Christy kept Kara from bolting while I pried the heavy door up, the hinges squealing in protest. I grabbed our reluctant hostage and dragged her down the ladder with me. Christy brought up the rear.

The subbasement was a large open area, more an extension of the sewer system than anything. It smelled of damp decay, and I couldn't help but notice that the stone walls and floor were scratched all to hell.

It was best not to consider what had made those.

"Follow me." I started toward what had once been the main tunnel access.

"Ouch!" a voice behind me hissed. Almost immediately, I had to blink as a white light filled the room. A ball of energy sprang from Christy's fingertips. Oh yeah, almost forgot I was the only one with night vision.

"That's better," she said, taking a look around. "Big rats, you said?"

"Really big ones."

"What the fuck?!" Kara shrieked, her eyes wide in the magical light.

"Newsflash, doll." I dragged her forward with me. "Your sister-in-law-to-be is a witch, not a bitch...that one's my job."

"Kara!" a voice cried from up above - Mark's. "*FIGHT THEM!!*"

Thankfully, I was ready for him. "*IGNORE THAT ASSHOLE!!*" It cost me, though. I staggered from the effort, but one consolation was that he was probably doing the same. Vamps our age weren't up to the task of a protracted compulsion tug-o-war with a human rope. With any luck, he wouldn't dare try again while in close pursuit of us - it would leave him vulnerable.

Gathering myself, I stepped forward to where I remembered the access grate to be and saw...nothing. Fuck!

Looking closer, I saw the vague outline of masonry work. They'd sealed it up with a cement plug. Jesus Christ, they really were scared of whatever was down here. I began to doubt the wisdom of my escape plan.

"Give it up, Lucinda!" Mark called. Behind us, several sets of feet began to descend the ladder. Shit!

"We're trapped," I said.

"Wanna bet?" Christy replied, turning back toward the trapdoor. A red glow enveloped her body, illuminating the room in bloody silhouettes - quite apt, considering the circumstances. It wasn't anything new for me, other than not being the target for a change, but it definitely freaked out the girl. Kara's eyes grew even wider and she looked like she was about to scream her head off.

Pity that I beat her to it.

"No!" I cried, the old me fighting her way to the surface once more. "Blow the wall...uh, you might not hit all of them." Goddamn, I really needed to get my head on straight.

Christy eyed me skeptically for a moment before turning and taking aim toward the wall in front of us.

"You have enough in you?" I asked.

"I guess we'll find out."

Kara let loose a whining cry to Mark, just as a rush of power sped from Christy's body. It slammed into the wall like a wrecking ball. The concrete shattered, sending smoke and dust billowing in our direction.

The girl's screams dissolved into choked coughs, which was a good thing for her sake. The concept of decking her and tossing her limp form over my shoulder had begun to creep into my mind. Unfortunately, that idea went right out the window as Christy dropped to one knee. The effort of moving the crates and, now this, had drained her already shaky batteries.

Fuck! When it rains, it pours...

Literally, it would seem. As the noise from the explosion subsided, the sound of distant rushing water hit my ears. The tunnels under Vegas were famous for their flash floods. Such was life in the desert. It was dry most of the time, but when it did rain, it came down like the wrath of God...or gods, in this case. This storm was anything but natural.

I shoved Kara forward. Looking down at Christy, I had a nanosecond to consider that not too long ago I would have gladly left her to whatever fate Mark had in store for her. Amazing what just a few months could do to a person. Hell, if push came to shove, I'd save her ass long before some other vamps...like, say, a certain redhead who had a boatload of pain coming her way the second I got back to New York.

I hauled Christy up and draped her arm over my shoulder. "You good to go?"

"Peachy," she replied weakly.

I took a step forward, then hesitated. Multiple scents caught my nose from up ahead: stagnant water, mold, decay, and something beneath it all...a pungent smell like someone had decided to fry up rotten eggs on a brimstone-fueled griddle.

"What's wrong?"

"Oh, nothing. Probably just a...ARGH!" Red-hot pain lanced my side a second before a thunderous explosion echoed in the room around us. The fuckers were armed, what a surprise.

"Kill them all!" a voice commanded from behind us through the smoke that continued to linger in the air. It was probably the only thing saving us from being riddled with holes. Sadly, Christy's little magic ball of light still hung in the air. Whatever cover we had wasn't all that good.

Biting my lip against the pain...a thirty-eight caliber from the feel of it - I dragged Christy forward. Thankfully, the bullet had just grazed me. As it was, it hurt like a motherfucker, but wasn't debilitating. My enhanced healing would deal with it soon enough.

Fortunately, the concept of possibly getting shot in all the confusion had sunk into Kara's head and she'd taken the hint. Moving ahead of us, at least to the edge of the light, she stepped into the tunnel.

The entryway opened up into the sewers about twenty feet ahead. Once through, I leaned Christy against the wall on one side and dragged the girl to the other with me.

"They shot at us!" she whined.

"Perceptive, ain't you?"

"They could have..."

"Hit you? Yeah, I'd suggest you remember that," I hissed back. "Now shut up!" I bent and grabbed a couple of fist-sized hunks of concrete from the ground. I didn't have a gun, but that didn't mean I couldn't be just as dangerous. Footsteps entered the tunnel behind us and I whipped a rock in the general direction, putting my vampiric strength behind it.

A scream of pain was my reward. Ah, gotta love that. I threw a few more and gunshots rang out in response along with the whine of bullets ricocheting off the walls. It was a standoff. They couldn't hit us, but as long as they were in the tunnel, I could barely miss.

At last, I heard the retreat of footsteps.

"Give us the girl, Lucinda," Mark called out. "I just want her. You and the witch can go. We won't follow."

What the fuck? Did he think I'd gone stupid in the past hour?

"See?" Kara asked, trying to weasel out of my grasp. "Let me go and they'll..."

"You really are your brother's sister, aren't you?"

"We can do this all day!" Christy called out from opposite me. She'd regained her composure, but was apparently all set to lose it again. She raised her arms and started chanting softly. What the hell? It was doubtful she had enough juice in her to send a ball of fiery death at our pursuers. The truth of the matter was some part of me still wasn't sure I wanted her to - a thought I was probably smart not to vocalize.

Christy finished what she was doing and slumped down again, breathing hard. I waited for something to blow up, but nothing happened. After a moment, she got back to her feet, using the wall to steady herself. "Let's go," she called out quietly.

I was about to question whether she'd just lost her mind, when I heard a voice call out from nowhere, "Step on out so I can knock someone else's head off!" It sounded nearly identical to my own. What the hell?

Christy smiled in the light of her magic glowball, then stepped away from the wall...or at least one of her did. I saw two Christies. One was crouched with her head peeking out toward the entrance. The other, standing there, waved me on.

"Let's go," the second one said. "It won't last long."

Dragging Kara with me, I stepped toward her, half expecting a hail of gunfire to follow our movement. When nothing happened, I looked back, only half surprised to see that another me had appeared in the same spot I'd been - some kind of illusion no doubt.

I let out a small laugh. "Let's go, kiddo."

In response, Kara screamed Mark's name at the top of her lungs.

I turned, balling a fist, but Christy said, "It's okay. That glamour will block sound from this side. But we need to move. I don't think they'll be fooled for long."

I nodded, but then remembered where we were. Magic or not, drawing attention to ourselves probably wasn't a good idea. Pulling Kara close, I got right in her face and bared my fangs. "Here's the deal. You know witches are real, and now you know vampires are, too. Want to know another secret? I'm pretty sure we're not the worst things down here. Keep your fucking mouth shut unless you want to meet whatever is."

Thankfully, the water hadn't reached our section of the tunnels yet. Marlene apparently had the good sense to build in some serious drainage runoffs in this area. Unfortunately, I didn't have a good feeling for what lay ahead. Even back during my tenure in this city, flash floods were known to carry away anyone unlucky enough to get caught in them. We needed to get far enough away to surface safely, but not so far that the floodwaters or the creatures who now ruled the underground could find us.

"What are we up against?" Christy asked.

"Not sure," I replied, "but Marlene was afraid of them. It's a safe bet that's not good news for us."

30

I knew the sewers of New York pretty well. Sadly, my knowledge of the Vegas tunnels was both incomplete and rusty. Thus, I made a best guess, trying to use my nose to pinpoint any wafts of fresh air that hit us - a losing proposition if ever there was one. The smell of those creatures, whatever they were, seemed to get stronger with every twist and turn.

I tried to keep us pointed toward the heart of the city. Coming out on the fringe of the desert wouldn't be great. Mark and his buddies could potentially mow us down out in the open if they caught us there. Bullets weren't typically lethal to vampires, but if one were to get lucky and blow a hole in the wrong place, it could be bad. And they were definitely on our tail.

Christy's illusion had bought a five, maybe ten-minute lead. Eventually, though, shots echoed through the tunnels, followed by voices shouting. Every few minutes afterward we'd hear some sound indicating they were still coming - although it soon became difficult to tell, even with my enhanced senses, just how close or far they were.

For our part, we kept as quiet as we could, speaking only in whispers - with the occasional threat to Kara when she looked like she was about to open her yap and scream. Christy kept her ball of light going, but had shrunk it so that it was just enough to illuminate the path. Sadly, judging by the strain on her face, it wasn't just to thwart our pursuers. She was nearly out of gas.

I took stock of our little band as we marched through the damp tunnel. We were going to be quite the scene once we surfaced. One of us was practically naked, and I looked like I'd just escaped from a slaughterhouse.

Another shot echoed through the sewers somewhere behind us, causing even me to jump. We doubled our pace and kept going, turning down another side tunnel to try to evade them.

"Why are they shooting at us?" Kara whined.

"They're not."

"Do you think they met up with those things you mentioned?" Christy asked.

"No, there'd be a lot more gunfire if that were the case."

"Then what?

"No idea, but if I had to guess, I'd say they're trying to drive us forward, keep us from doubling back. The longer we're down here during this storm, the better chance we have of running into whatever it is we don't want to meet."

We continued on in silence for a while, stopping only for Christy to catch her breath. Though her pregnancy wasn't that far along, our forced march through the sewers was definitely taking a toll on her.

"What's that?" Christy asked.

There was a slight rise ahead, and it appeared something blocked the way. Moving closer, I could see it was a filthy curtain strung up between the sides of the tunnel. I described it to my companions.

"People?" Hope crept its way into Christy's voice. "Think they'll know a way out?"

"I have a feeling they don't know anything right now," I muttered, stepping forward. I approached the curtain and pulled it aside. A humble living space lay before us. It was small, damp, and dingy, but livable nevertheless. Plastic bins stood off to one side full of old clothes. There was a desk with two small chairs. A ramshackle bunk bed was on one side. Various broken toys lay about, suggesting a family had called this place home...once. The scent of dried blood lingered.

I'd been lucky, despite being young and stupid when I first came here. My former apartment had been little more than a drafty closet. Even so, I'd managed to keep my head above water. I had a job, a roof over my head, and a boyfriend who adored me. It wasn't much, but there'd been a sense of satisfaction to it all. If I'd stopped to realize how much I truly had to lose, perhaps things would have ended differently. I might have turned down the offer to work at Pandora's Box and continued to enjoy my simple life.

No! That was too easy to imagine. Colin had marked me from a young age. Sooner or later, I'd have wound up in my current situation.

"Sally?" Christy asked from behind me.

"Huh?"

"Are you okay? You kind of zoned out there."

"Yeah."

"These people aren't coming back, are they?"

"They never stood a chance," I replied, only partially referring to their ultimate fate.

"Come on. Let's go. If whatever took them is..."

"MARK!"

Oh shit! We both turned and watched as Kara, the stupid little fuck, ran off down the tunnel screaming the name of someone she wrongly thought was trying to rescue her.

"You must really love Tom to go through all this shit for that little bitch."

"Well, yeah," Christy replied, panting as she tried to keep up.

"No misgivings about sitting around the holidays with that girl for the rest of your life?"

"I'm used to people with attitude."

"*Touché.*"

Considering she was running in the dark through a wet tunnel and wearing nothing but her underwear, Kara led us on a merry little chase - albeit it didn't help that Christy wasn't quite up for a long-distance sprint. I could've gone on ahead and caught up to the little twat, but I found myself reluctant to leave my traveling companion. Something about the abandoned toys back in that makeshift dwelling had unnerved me.

Goddamn, I must really be going soft. If this kept up, I'd be crocheting baby blankets by the end of the week.

Well, okay, my feelings weren't entirely because of Christy growing on me or because I didn't care to see her eviscerated in her current condition. The truth was that if Marlene had been afraid of whatever was down here, then that was worrisome. Vampires didn't freak out easily...at least those that weren't complete dumbasses.

Sure, plenty of vamps were afraid of Bill, but they fell into that latter category. Hell, I'd barely blinked when facing down a monstrous Sasquatch up in Northern Canada. Yet down here in strange tunnels with a supernatural storm brewing overhead, I found myself shaken. Hah, some big bad monster I'd turned out to be.

"What's the plan now?" she asked.

"We find her and get the fuck out of here."

"Once again..."

"Yeah, yeah, I know. You could have thought of that."

"What about Mark?"

"Fuck him. He's not worth it."

"It would be better if we killed him, you know."

"I know."

"For what he did to Kara."

"Uh huh."

"And what he did to you."

"Oh," I mused, "what did he do to me?"

"Come on, Sally," she huffed. "I'm not stupid. Are you telling me it's coincidence that he came all the way out east for Kara alone? That it was just dumb chance that she also happened to be connected to you in a six-degrees-of-Kevin-Bacon way?"

"It's possible." I forged ahead, feeling her silent stare dig in between my shoulder blades. "Well, maybe not probable."

"I thought so...whoa!" She slipped on the wet concrete. My reflexes immediately took over and I spun to steady her. "Thanks."

"Don't mention it." I turned a corner, following Kara's scent. "Crap!"

Here, the water level was rising fast. Whereas the most we'd had to deal with up to then had been a few puddles, it looked like we'd be wading the rest of the way.

"Are you sure she went this way?"

"I can smell her cheap perfume."

"Mark and the others?"

"Hard to tell."

"Do you still care about him?"

The question caught me off guard, and for just a moment I hesitated. I was tempted to throw back some lie or bit of snark, but down here in the darkness with the open sky seemingly miles away, my sense of sarcasm waned. "He was a good man once."

"He's not anymore. You know that, right?"

"I know."

"But still..."

Yeah, that was the kicker. He was a cold-blooded killer bent on a revenge that was utterly pointless for no other reason than empty satisfaction. But had I been all that different? I'd killed countless people, most of them with a smile on my face. I'd hardened my heart and let it shrivel up into an icy ball of coal. Even now, I found myself with few qualms about erasing those who got in my way.

And yet...

Little by little, that humanity inside of me, the one that James had told me to search for - which I hadn't believed was still alive - started to open its eyes and take a look around. What it saw wasn't pretty, but it seemed it didn't quite want to go back to the grave from which it had crawled. Couldn't the same be true of Mark? Maybe he just needed a push, a reminder that there was still some good in him.

Maybe...

An angry hiss sounded at us from out of nowhere, snapping me back to the present, and ending my tortured internal debate. I wasn't sure whether to be terrified or relieved.

Either way, whatever it was that Marlene had been afraid of, we were about to meet it.

31

It was as if a section of the wall began to move. One moment it was solid rock, and the next it was a writhing mass of darkness. It disengaged from its spot and dropped into the knee-deep water where it rose up and took shape.

It was humanoid, but only in the vaguest of sense. About my height, but twice as wide, it stood on squat legs upon which rested a thick, nearly cylindrical body. Arms extended from it that ended in clubs made of the same stony material that comprised the rest of it. A misshapen head topped it off. Glowing orange eyes stared hollowly at me, but it was the mouth that drew my full attention. It grinned with wicked, obsidian teeth - the same smile I'd seen in the casino the day before. Obviously these things were shape shifters of a sort, able to blend in - mostly - with humans. Also obvious was that down here, the thing didn't feel the need to play dress up.

"We don't want any trouble," I said, backing up.

To my surprise, a gravelly voice replied, "*We do.*" Not exactly a promising answer.

"Be thou fae or demon," Christy said from my side, "know that I am a Magi, neutral in your war. This vampire is here with me under protection of truce. Let us pass and there shall be no transgression."

I looked sideways at her. It was hokey, but still better than anything I had. Hell, if it worked, I wasn't above letting a little diplomacy save my ass.

"*Truce? War?*" it gurgled as it advanced a step. "*We know not of such. Slept we have in the deep for age beyond count. Now we awaken. Something calls to us.*"

"Something called to you? What? By the provisions set forth in the Humbaba Accord, I demand you identify your allegiance."

"All that's in there?" I asked, referencing the ancient treaty, now broken, that once kept the darker forces of the world from tearing each other apart.

"Of course. Didn't you read it?"

"I was waiting for the movie."

Fortunately, our mineral-encrusted *friend* saved me from further embarrassment. "*Accord? Allegiance? We serve only ourselves. We take what we wish. We wish for this city.*"

"Good luck," I said as it shambled forward. "The tourism board is gonna probably have a few words to say about..."

One of the club-like appendages shot forward, cutting my pithy reply short. It wasn't wholly unexpected, but still faster than I'd have thought a pile of granite could move. I brought up an arm to block and lost a hunk of skin as its arm grazed mine. Fuck!

It was like fighting something covered in broken glass.

It swung the other club, but this time I saw it coming. I ducked and sidestepped.

Christy backed up and raised her arms in a familiar gesture. She meant to blast this thing to hell. I just hoped she had enough juice left to get the job done - and quickly, too. With me out of its immediate way, the creature went after her, not being overly discerning about which of us it killed first.

Once upon a time, I'd have saved my own ass and let her keep the thing busy with her death throes. A part of me almost wished I was still like that. Fuck that whole growing as a person thing.

I balled my fist and drove it into the creature's back, mentally promising myself to give Bill two ass-kickings if he ever showed his face around me again.

I got lucky, if one considered a possible broken hand lucky. The creature's midsection was ever so slightly more pliable than its arms had been. Even so, it was like punching a brick wall. Luckily for me, vamps tend to be strong enough to do things like that.

The creature let out a grunt and spun its head one hundred and eighty degrees to face me - neat trick. Its wicked teeth, far larger than my fangs, were inches from my face. One good chomp and I'd receive the mother of all facelifts.

I didn't want to wait and see what other feats of contortion this abomination had up its sleeve. I wrapped my arms around its torso and craned my head back as far as possible to avoid the worst French kiss in the history of smooching.

I lifted...ugh! I'm no lightweight, despite my size. I can rip the door right off a Cadillac, yet this thing barely budged on my first attempt.

"Get out of the way!" Christy shouted.

"In a second," I grunted, giving another heave. The beast finally left the floor, just as I reached the limits of my strength. I fell back, throwing it over my head. I landed in the water and submerged, but even so, still felt the impact its body made as it landed behind me.

I tried to sit up, but a foot planted me back down in the unsanitary stew. What the fuck?

A moment later, the water heated up, nearly painfully so. I was about to become a scalded lobster when the foot stepped off and a hand pulled me up. I grabbed hold, but we stumbled and I plopped down again. Blinking the muck out of my eyes, I found Christy sitting in front of me, breathing hard. "I was hoping for a hot bath tonight, but not quite what I had in mind."

"What the hell was that?" I asked, splashing some slime her way.

"Sorry," she gasped. "Didn't want to hit you by accident."

Oh yeah. I stood up and saw the water around us turn brownish from all the blood that had washed off me. It wasn't really an improvement. I'd take sticky over slimy any day of the week.

The creature lay face down, smoking. Its body was mostly intact, and it shuddered once. I backed up a step, but that was all the movement it made. It appeared the heat had fused it together.

"Didn't want to waste time trying to find a soft spot," Christy said from behind me.

I turned and offered her a helping hand. "Good call."

"Thanks. Let's hope we don't meet any more. I don't think I have another shot like that in me."

"I didn't think you had that one."

"Almost didn't."

"Horseshoes and hand grenades." I was glad that we didn't have to find out what would have happened had she not.

The water was now up to our waists and a current had begun to push at us. The storm must have been dumping a lot of rain above. It wouldn't be long before a raging torrent of fast-moving water would flood the tunnels. If we didn't find Kara and get out before then, she was done for. Back during my days here, there were stories every year of bodies found in the drainage tunnels after the rains came.

Thankfully, we hadn't yet run into any more of those things, but I had a feeling that, much like the water, their presence in these tunnels would soon be impossible to avoid. Though most of the smell around us was the flood plucking shit off the walls and floor, their scent was still heavy in the air.

"Are you sure she came this way?"

"I'm not sure of anything other than the flight out of here had better have a fucking shower."

"What about the..."

A scream echoed in the tunnels ahead. It was definitely Kara's.

"Hold on to me," I ordered and began pushing my way ahead. Every step brought us a little deeper. By the time we reached a curve in the tunnel, even I could barely keep my pace. Soon we'd have to swim, and that would be about as effective as waiting for shit to slide uphill. Fortunately, though, we vampires have a few tricks up our sleeves for just such an emergency.

Sidling close to the wall, I extended my claws and dug them into the concrete for purchase. "Ouch! Watch the hair."

Christy held on for dear life as I slowly made my way forward, my feet at last losing contact with the ground. Drowning isn't too much of a problem for those of us who are already dead, but the witch piggybacking on me might've taken issue with it. There was also the fact that I really didn't want to be submerged under Las Vegas's collective shit water.

"When we find her," I called back, "I hope you don't mind if I kick her ass for running."

"Be my guest. I can always wipe her mind later."

I smiled despite the unpleasantness of the situation. When this was all over, I might even consider hanging out with Christy more often...sans her boyfriend and his family, of course.

I continued to crawl forward, each handhold bringing me closer to the limits of my strength. I had nearly reached it when the tide finally began to slacken. I craned my neck. Maybe we were heading up an incline, but it was hard to see with my head just barely above water.

Kara's cry for help came again, seemingly just up ahead...although it was difficult to tell. Christy and I kept quiet. There was no telling if she'd do something stupid if she found out we were the ones coming to her rescue.

I continued to claw my way ahead, easier now, when I realized too late why that was.

A cross current slammed into us from the T-intersection we reached and ripped my grip from the wall, catapulting us through the water at a ninety-degree angle. Christy's hold on me slipped, and she let out a cry as she was swept away down the new tunnel.

I reached to try and grab her, but was slammed head-first into the opposite wall before being dragged under.

32

I saw stars, or at least would have, had a glop of something unpleasant not been washed into my face. Oh yeah, I was definitely going to kick Kara's ass when this was over and done with. Victim or not, the girl had earned it.

I dug my claws into the wall and began to climb, heading up on a diagonal so as to not get immediately swept away. Even so, it was a struggle against the current. I hoped Christy was okay, but pushed my worry for her to the side. She was a smart girl. No doubt she'd kept a little magic in reserve for a life or death emergency such as...oh, I don't know, being caught up in a biblical deluge of storm runoff and sewer sludge. If not, there wasn't much I could do about it.

I finally surfaced, grasping a hold of the corner opposite of the one I'd been dragged from. Hopefully, like the previous tunnel, the current in this one would be less powerful. Dragging myself around the corner,

I saw the tunnel rise ahead of me. There was perhaps a foot, no more than two, of space between the rushing water and the ceiling here, but up ahead, things were different.

The tunnel opened up further on, the top rising high above. Machinery hummed in the distance, but I couldn't see its source. I must've been in a pumping station or something. A metal catwalk suspended from the ceiling ran into the distance, hanging just above the surface of the water.

Oh, and look at what the catwalk dragged in. Hanging by her fingers, the majority of her body in the water, was Kara. She held tight, but lacked the strength to pull herself up...wuss.

I ducked below the surface and began to claw my way to her...making headway now that the tide of the cross tunnel was behind me. It was a good thing, too. I had a feeling things were only going to get worse. The water level still seemed to be rising. It was only a matter of time before a tsunami of storm runoff came rushing through here. When that happened, it wouldn't matter which tunnel we were in.

Sadly, the sediment - or at least I tried to convince myself it was sediment - made it impossible for even my enhanced vision to cut through the murky water. I had to rely on my best guestimate. Finally reaching what I thought to be a spot right behind her, I surfaced and, of course, found nothing. Goddamnit!

Not one to look a gift catwalk in the mouth, I grabbed hold of the railing and hoisted myself out of the filthy water. God, what I wouldn't have given for a bar of soap.

I coughed and took my first dry breath in what felt like hours. The scents it brought told me too late that I was not alone.

BLAM

The bullet slammed home into my shoulder and nearly sent me tumbling back into the flood. I should have let it - a second ball of hot lead caught me in the gut and drove me to my knees.

I looked up to see Barlow step out from a side tunnel I'd missed from my vantage point down below. He grinned like the shaved ape he was and held a smoking weapon.

Mark walked past him, one arm draped protectively around Kara. I had little doubt he'd planned it that way. It wasn't hard to imagine him using her like bait until such time as he saw me coming, then swooping in to save the day. It's exactly what I would have done.

"Hi, lover," I gasped, spitting up blood.

"I won't lie, Lucinda," he replied, "you've looked better." He took a sniff and wrinkled his brow. "Smelled better, too. I hate to say it, but I think I'm going to pass on our date."

"At least you didn't waste any money buying flowers."

"Kill her, Mark!" Kara whined, burying her head in his shoulder. "She's a monster."

She was right about that, but too stupid to realize I wasn't the only one.

"Tsk tsk." He stroked her hair with one hand. "Let's not be hasty."

"You should cap her, boss," Barlow suggested, "so we can get the fuck out of here. Marlene wouldn't want us to stay down..."

Mark turned and grinned savagely. "Who gives a shit? Marlene's dead. That means I'm in charge now. So I would kindly ask you to shut the fuck up while I'm speaking."

"Not much of a coven left to rule." I was trying to buy time for my body to heal up enough to do something, albeit I wasn't sure what. Barlow still had his weapon trained on me and, no doubt, had plenty of ammunition left. My reflexes were superior, but the distance between us meant he could pepper me with lead before I closed in on him.

"The others are around somewhere," Mark mused.

"You split up?"

"I needed someone to be a distraction for those things. Don't worry. They're all big boys. I'm sure they're fine...and if not, I'll just make more."

"What do you mean, Mark?" Kara asked, lifting her head.

"You just don't get it, you stupid little cooze, do you?"

She recoiled as if he'd slapped her in the face. I had to admit it was strange for me, too. It was hard to reconcile the man who stood before me with the one I had known all those years ago. He'd been kind, never one to let the seedy underbelly of the Strip get him down. Many a night we'd spent together doing little more than confiding our dreams and enjoying each other's company.

The creature before me wore his face, but that was all. Even that illusion didn't last. Mark pulled out a lighter and flicked it on, illuminating the dark space - no doubt for Kara's benefit. His eyes darkened and his fangs extended. "Lucinda's not the only monster down here, girl. She's not even the worst."

I would have said something pithy at that, but Kara's screams drowned out whatever comment I could make. The poor, dumb girl. It sucked to be the last one to get the memo.

He grabbed her by the hair before she could back away. It wasn't much, but it was possibly my only chance. I sprang at both of them. The impact would probably shatter a few of her bones, but it was better than what he had planned for her.

Sadly, I'd momentarily forgotten about Barlow. Another shot rang out, echoing even above the roar of rushing water. I might have noticed it had grown noticeably louder had it not been for the sensation of my left kneecap being blown apart.

Fuck me! As an experienced vamp, my pain threshold was pretty damn high, but that didn't mean I didn't feel it. First gut shot, and now crippled. These assholes were going for maximum hurt.

That was bad for me, but maybe it wasn't the smartest course of action for them. The fuckwits were making the same mistake Marlene had. If you have the chance, kill your enemy. Otherwise, your enemy is going to fucking shiv you the first chance she gets.

Assuming she gets a chance, that is.

For now, I settled for crashing down onto the metal grate that held us. I don't weigh much - not bragging or anything, although I do work to keep my figure - but the catwalk noticeably shuddered as I landed with a splash, the water level seeping up over the bottom.

Mark smiled down at me as he pulled the still screaming Kara in. He pushed her head to the side and flashed his fangs at me. At the last second, though, he shifted and bit down onto her shoulder instead. The bone made an audible crunch.

The pitch of her cries increased to the point where wine glasses somewhere above us were surely shattering. It's times like this that I rued the fact that earplugs weren't part of my normal ensemble.

Mark pulled back and licked his lips. The wound on her shoulder was ugly, but not fatal. "Sorry, baby, but you're just not worth turning. Sluts like you are a dime a dozen. Wouldn't you agree, Lucinda?"

I glared up at him, mindful of Barlow's gun still trained upon me. Part of me was waiting for the perfect moment. The rest was in shock at how far Mark had fallen, how much he'd let the predator inside take over.

Had I ever been that bad? It was a stupid question. I knew the answer.

"I'm still gonna have some fun with you, though..." Before he could finish, the sound of rushing water became louder until it all but drowned him out.

A wave struck us. The surge was at least four feet higher than the top of the water had previously been. It hit Barlow and Mark from behind, dousing the lighter and staggering them, before completely covering me.

I tensed my good leg. There wasn't going to be a better time.

The moment the surge passed, I launched myself. Barlow fired another shot, but this one went wide, thanks to the small tidal wave of filth. I slammed into Mark and drove him backward into his pet goon, ruining any shot he had unless he planned to shoot me through Mark - a dubious premise. It would have been a smart maneuver, one I'd have done in a second, but I doubted he had either the brains or the balls to empty a clip into his new master.

Mark lost his grip on Kara, who fell to her knees whimpering in the renewed darkness. Jeez, she just had a little nip taken out of her. *I* was the one missing a fucking kneecap.

Unfortunately for me, this served to free up both of Mark's hands.

I managed to reach past him with my left, knocking the gun out of Barlow's grasp and into the raging water below. I raked the nails of my right hand across Mark's chest, drawing a furrow of blood. Unfortunately, he extended his own claws and brought them up into my abdomen, right into the spot where I'd been shot. Fuck! It had just started to close up, too. In a split second, he undid what little healing my body had managed and then dug even farther in.

The pain was incredible, and I screamed despite myself. Mark wrapped his free arm around me, drawing me in closer as if in an embrace. Barlow, showing he had a few working brain cells, grabbed the hand I'd used to disarm him and did the same, preventing my escape.

As I opened my mouth to cry out again, Mark pressed his lips into mine.

He then pulled back and flexed the fingers of the hand still inside of me. "I always wanted to make you scream, Lucinda. This is not quite how I imagined it happening, but I'll take it. I hope it's good for you, too."

I felt woozy. Mark's hand continued to tear at my innards. A few more inches and he'd be in prime condition to rip the very heart from my body.

A voice inside my head reminded me that I'd broken his heart once upon a time. Perhaps this was a fitting comeuppance.

I was in dire straits. A small part of me even hoped that Kara finally took the hint. This was the point in a sappy romantic drama where the jilted lover would grow a set and rise up to strike down her tormentor. Alas, that shit only happens in the movies. I was in a bad place, and the only way out was to rely on the one person I could - *myself.*

My head lolled back and my eyelids fluttered, only partially of my own volition. My insides dripped out in great globules from the wound in my stomach.

There was no way I was going to be able to take much more.

"Hey now, baby," Mark chided, "you're not supposed to fall asleep until it's all ov...ARGH!"

I drove my head forward and felt the satisfying crunch of his nose breaking.

Before either of us could do anything about it, we were both underwater again as another surge swept into us. It wouldn't be long now before this tunnel was completely flooded.

It also wouldn't be long now for me. The disgusting water filled with the scent of my blood. I could only imagine the unsanitary things filling my body's open cavity.

Fuck that! No way was I going out like this. The end of the world was coming and I, for one, wanted to be around to see it.

We continued to struggle in the deluge against both the current and one another. The murky water had one advantage - it left everything good and slippery. The wave subsided and I yanked back my left arm just as my head surfaced again. Barlow lost his grip, and I used my newly freed appendage to pull Mark's arm from my body.

It was a good effort - it just wasn't enough. Though we might've been on equal terms on any other given day, I was wounded badly. He pushed me back and my ruined leg gave way.

I went to one knee and was rewarded with an uppercut to the chin, sending me down to the floor of the catwalk, now inches below the rising waterline.

I rolled onto my back and looked up. Mark

grinned down at me in the darkness with Barlow standing beside him. Off to one side, Kara sat motionless against the wall - coughing out water and being more or less useless.

I tried to think of my remaining options and came up empty.

Mark's foot buried itself in my midsection and I let out a gasp of pain that found me choking on a combination of floodwater and my own blood.

So this was it? Not quite how I envisioned checking out.

I blinked sludge from my eyes, and saw Mark's smile had grown even wider. He began to unbuckle his belt. He meant to have his pound of flesh, and there wasn't a goddamned thing I could do about it. Oh well, at least I wouldn't enjoy it. That would show him.

Just then, something caught my eye. I glanced past them, surprised. The orange light of the morning sun filtered in from far above through what must have been a manhole or grate.

Huh. I hadn't realized so much time had passed, nor would I have guessed that the storm had ended, judging by the epic flood surrounding us.

"Any chance you want to share her with me, boss?" Barlow asked as more dim sunlight appeared above their heads.

"Why not?" Mark replied over his shoulder. "Consider it your first fringe benefit under my regime."

Multiple dots of daylight blinked above them. Maybe there was a chance after all. If I could grab them both with the last of my strength, maybe I could hold them long enough for a few stray rays to hit us down here. It was a long shot and wouldn't end well for me, but at least we'd all go out in a blaze of...

Wait a second. That wasn't sunlight up above.

Sunlight doesn't blink.

I focused my gaze and saw the ceiling undulate as at least three of those rock creatures disengaged from it. One of them turned toward me and, for just a second, a mockery of flesh replaced the rocky skin of its face. It smiled an obsidian grin at me...the same face I'd seen in the casino the night before.

Mark must have noticed my look of shock, because he turned - albeit not before planting a boot in my chest to keep me put. Smart. Marlene had taught him well after all.

Smart, but sadly not fast enough. The creatures launched themselves at us. One landed on Barlow and immediately buried its granite-like teeth into his shoulder. It tore loose a mound of his flesh as they both tumbled over the catwalk railing and into the water below.

A familiar flash of light from beneath the surface momentarily lit up the room. The asshole had met his well-deserved fate.

Mark, however, was both smarter and tougher than his henchman. He sidestepped and shoved one of the creatures over into the torrent below. The third, my *friend* from the other night, had landed with the apparent intent of finishing me off, but turned instead toward the greater threat. Under different circumstances I might have been insulted, but decided to let it slide just this once.

Mark and the beast grappled while I summoned the last of my strength to roll out of the way. I backpedaled and found myself next to Kara. We were both a mess, just in different ways. At least I had the advantage of seeing what was going on.

A high-pitched keening sound escaped her lips as I brushed against her, her brain apparently having been pushed into overload. That was one advantage her brother had on her. He'd grown up on dorky shit. The sight before us would have probably just given him a hard-on.

Great! *There* was an image I didn't need stuck in my head.

Another wave struck the catwalk and it shuddered. Things were definitely getting worse - not that they were all that good to begin with. We were probably minutes at most away from being completely underwater.

If the creature won, I was fucked. If Mark won, I was likewise fucked - probably literally.

The girl was useless as anything but a paperweight at this point. Thus, there was only one possible solution to this problem - me. What a surprise.

Bracing my good leg beneath my body, I began to inch my way back to a standing position. I almost didn't make it. As Mark continued to struggle with the shape shifter, I almost fell on my ass - twice. My left leg refused to support my weight, its healing no doubt retarded by the blood still spurting out of my body.

By the time I did make it up, using the wall as support, I was even more lightheaded. Forget coke - there's nothing like a near-mortal wound to produce a killer high.

The thought of cocaine brought with it memories of Jeff, though. He'd been responsible for nearly all of this...a chain reaction on legs. Thinking of him, Colin's betrayal, and all the things that had been done to me as a result, brought with it a wave of anger to rival the storm surge. My eyes flashed to black and my head momentarily cleared.

There was no time to waste - I had the feeling I wouldn't get another second wind.

I hobbled forward to where the creature was slowly forcing Mark back. He was pressed up against the railing of the catwalk, the rock monster's back to me as it tried to lean in and give him one hell of a hickey.

I stumbled as I finally reached them, but that was fine. Neither had noticed me close the gap. They'd regret disregarding me as a threat.

I grasped the creature from the bottom and heaved with everything I had to give, using my good leg as leverage. Ugh! The fucking thing weighed a ton. I barely managed it, but that was good enough for the accounting.

Both combatants, locked in a death struggle, flipped over the edge.

The creature tumbled into the water below, but

Mark was both lighter and more agile. He twisted out of the monster's grasp and was able to grab hold of the railing with one hand. He hung partly in the rushing water while I watched, unsure whether to be glad or horrified. Looking up at me, he smiled a predatory grin as he started to pull himself up. Guess he wasn't quite ready to let bygones be bygones.

I didn't have much left to fight back with, but then again, maybe I didn't need much. His grin became a whole lot less smug as I slammed the claws of my hand into the back of his.

"You fucking whore!"

"For the last time, I was just a dancer!" I spat, tired of being called that.

He reached up with his free arm. That's when I saw the lights from below. Orange eyes rose up from beneath him. Their glow cut through even the murk of the water. I've seen some messed up shit in my time, but the sight below chilled even me to the bone.

I could only stare, wide-eyed, as they burst from the water around Mark. Arms made of razor-sharp rock wrapped around his body. One of the creatures bit into his side, taking a hunk of flesh as if it were some sort of supernatural shark.

Mark let loose a scream of pain. The shock on his face mirrored that from when I had attacked him all those years ago. In that moment, my heart broke. All of this...every single moment...was my fault.

"Help me!" he cried. Instinctively, I pulled my claws from his hand and grasped his wrist instead.

"Please, Lucinda!"

I looked down at him and felt the disparate

worlds inside of my head collide. Christy was right. He did look a bit like Bill...

That's when things began to grind to a halt for me.

He looked like Bill, but he wasn't. Mark had once been a decent man, but he'd let the beast inside bury all that was good about him. He'd given in to the anger, the need for vengeance.

Bill had only been a vampire for a short while, but in that time, he'd seen more than some vamps a hundred times his age. Through it all, he'd somehow managed to stay himself. Whether it was his friends, his family, or his fucking dorky sensibility, he continually fought and won against his darker half. Not only that, but he'd somehow managed to drag me along for the ride.

The creatures continued to swarm Mark. He tried to fight back, but one pinned his other arm, and they began to drag him down. My grip began to slip under the weight. I needed to...

"Help me, Lu," he pleaded. "I never stopped loving you."

Thanks to Bill, I had been pulled back into the light...but only partially. There was a part of me that had tasted the darkness and liked it...a part I wasn't quite ready to give up yet, if ever. That part of me was strong, a survivor...a woman who would never again let others manipulate her.

That wasn't all, though. She was also a monster.

I heard the deceit in his voice, saw the lie behind his frightened eyes. The little girl in me stepped willingly aside. This was a man who had kidnapped an innocent woman, all in the name of petty revenge.

"Lucinda died a long time ago. My name is Sally."

I let go.

33

1981

"Quit your fucking whining and let's go," Night Razor growled.

I shrank back from him. "We don't have to do this, master. I'll try harder. I promise."

He turned toward me, his eyes darkening with annoyance. "See, that's exactly the problem. *I'll try harder, I promise*," he mocked. "We are the lords of the night. We own this town and everything in it. You disgust me. I had high hopes when I dragged you out of that whorehouse in Vegas. Figured I'd have to put a leash on you to keep you from cutting a swath through humanity. Instead, you sit there like a mouse every night. I swear to God if you weren't such a good lay, I'd have staked you myself by now."

I stood there and took the abuse. Every bit of it was true. The thing was, I deserved it. I was in Hell, and I deserved it. Not a night went by when the faces of those I killed didn't stare back at me from the shadows, haunting me: Minnie, Tina, and poor Mark. I'd killed more since then, all at Night Razor's insistence. It was either them or me. I hated myself, but was afraid of truly dying more...or more precisely, what Night Razor would do to me before letting me die.

"Is everything all right?" the man behind the desk, the night watchman of this apartment building, no doubt, asked us.

"My boyfriend and I were just here to visit my sister," I replied, disgusted at the lie. Night Razor was about as much a boyfriend as Marlene had been my mother. Both of them were monsters, each of whom had claimed domain over me in their own way.

"Oh?" the man replied, his tone doubtful. "And her name would be?"

He was probably hoping to trip us up, give him a reason to throw us out. I was tempted to say a fake name, let him kick us to the curb, but that would've just made Night Razor even madder. "Linda Carlsbad."

"Okay then," he replied, semi mollified but still distrusting. "I'll call her and let her know you're coming up."

Before he even finished the sentence, he'd signed his own death warrant. Faster than even my enhanced reflexes could follow, Night Razor crossed the distance between them. His hand closed upon the man's neck and squeezed, instantly cutting off his air. The watchman clawed at him in silent protest, but there was nothing he could do against such power.

Thankfully, it didn't last long. His eyes bulged and his struggles weakened. At last, he went still. Night

Razor gave the man's head a twist, snapping his neck more for amusement than any other reason. He then gently sat the watchman down, folding his arms below him as if he were asleep.

"There," he replied happily. Killing always put the sick son of a bitch in a better mood. "Now, where were we?"

It was my fault that we were there. Betty...*Firebird* had taken to the nightlife, as we called it, like a fish to water. She hadn't held a grudge against me for turning her, and in fact, had been ecstatic to have discovered she was stronger, faster, and would keep her good looks forever. I, on the other hand, was having trouble letting go, embracing my new *life,* as Night Razor called it.

Upon arriving in New York, I'd immediately purloined some recent issues of the *Las Vegas Sun* from the public library in the hopes of learning anything of the aftermath of my rampage. At the very least, I'd hoped to find Mark's obituary, reading that his loved ones were there when he was laid to rest. That would have given me some comfort. Sadly, there was no news of the kind. It was like the people I had murdered simply vanished straight off the face of the planet. As if they'd never even existed.

In my desperation, I'd placed a postcard in the mail addressed to my parents. It wasn't much - just a note that I was okay along with the address of where I lived now, a place the others referred to simply as "the loft".

I hadn't expected much in return, and I wasn't disappointed. The following year, I received a curt

Christmas card from my mother. "Season's Greetings - Mom" was all it read. I kept it under my pillow for weeks until I became scared of it being discovered. Night Razor didn't tolerate anyone keeping ties to their old lives.

Then it happened. Just a few weeks ago, I had received a letter from my sister. It was short and impersonal, letting me know she had gotten a job as a sales manager for some toy company and had moved to the city. She wasted little time in gloating how well she was doing and ended with a seemingly insincere hope that we'd get together for lunch at some point.

My mistake had been not destroying it immediately. In truth, it made me sick. She'd always been Daddy's girl, living up to his ideals. In the end, though, it had all been bullshit. She was now a successful, single career woman, probably willing to spit in the face of any man who wished her barefoot and pregnant. My only solace was knowing it had probably given my father an ulcer.

Sadly, that one bit of dark humor had been my undoing. Night Razor eventually found it and was furious. I had required nearly a full day to heal from his wrath. In the end, I'd promised to not follow up on it, a promise I had every intention of keeping.

Since then, I'd tried to be a better vampire. I'd thought maybe we'd moved past it, but tonight, he'd gotten some bug up his ass. Unbeknownst to me, he'd saved the letter. He dragged me from the loft, telling me it was time to grow up once and for all. It was time to embrace the new me, including the ridiculous name I'd been saddled with. Time for me to bury the past.

It was that last part that terrified me.

"Do it," he whispered as we stood in front of her apartment door. It was a nice building, much better than the shabby place I'd rented in Vegas. Standing there, I couldn't help but feel a glimmer of resentment simmering inside of me. For a moment, it nearly overpowered the fear I was feeling for Linda and for myself. She'd never been much of a sister to me, but she was my sister nevertheless. I didn't want anything bad to happen to her. I loved her.

Didn't I?

"***DO IT!!***"

The compulsion was subtle, almost a whisper in the back of my head. It was just a nudge. Unlike most of the other orders he'd given me, I felt I could have disobeyed this one. It was, no doubt, a test.

Fear won out and I raised my hand to knock. For several seconds, there was no response. I began to hope she wasn't home, but then I heard the footsteps. They were soft, easily missed by human ears. If I heard them, though, then Night Razor certainly did. A glance out of the corner of my eye confirmed the predatory grin on his face. God, how I hated him.

"I'm coming," a bored voice said from within. There was a pause and my sensitive eyes picked up the slightest variation in light behind the peephole in the door. My unnatural hearing registered a sharp intake of breath from the other side.

The bolt pulled back and a chain disengaged. The door opened, a bit too quickly had I been an unknown knocker. Linda was older, more mature than I remembered, but then it had been about five years since we'd last seen each other. She'd held up well. Her hair was up and she was wearing a robe over a pair of silk pajamas. Her face had filled out a bit and a natural beauty had replaced the teenaged good looks I remembered. She actually could have been one of the fashion models I used to unfavorably compare her to. Despite being four years older than me, she could have passed for nearly my age. Albeit, a small voice in the back of my mind corrected, she was physically now six years older, and the gap between us would keep growing as I no longer aged. She would eventually fade, where I would not. That was small comfort, however.

Though it was obvious she'd recognized me through the peephole, she put on a faux surprised face that was, no doubt, for my benefit. "Lucinda? Is that you?"

For a moment, my mouth refused to open. She had no idea what I was. If she did, she'd have slammed the door shut and dialed the police as fast as her fingers could move. Instead, I replied, "Hey, sis. It's been a long time."

"Let me look at you!" she said cheerfully enough. Her long, slender fingers wrapped around my shoulders as she examined me at arm's length. Anger welled in me from her touch. How dare she, after all this time!

I pushed it away, though, as her eyes took me in. My hair hung at shoulder length. I'd left a little body in it, but not nearly as much as seemed to be fashionable these days. I wore a simple sundress. I liked them because of the irony of their name. Night Razor was partial to me wearing them, too, but only because they were easy to remove. The only makeup I wore was some light lipstick and blush, toned down from my days as a dancer - a time I was now eager to forget.

Mild disapproval passed through Linda's eyes, once more igniting a spark inside of me. Her tone, though, remained pleasant. "You look simply delicious."

I was half surprised Night Razor didn't burst out laughing. "You look great, too," I said. "City life agrees with you."

"Doesn't it?" She drank in the compliment as if it were a cosmopolitan. "And who is this fine upstanding young man at your side?" Her eyes turned to Night Razor. His somewhat base attire, ripped jeans and a tight t-shirt, met with no such distaste from her. Her eyes greedily devoured his form and were obviously hungry for more.

"This is....my boyfriend, Jeff."

"Boyfriend, eh? A pleasure, Jeff." He simply nodded in response. "You've done well for yourself, Lucinda. How did you two meet?"

"We met on the job," Night Razor teased. "S...Lucinda works for me."

Linda passed a sly glance between us. It was obvious what she was thinking: *Poor, pathetic Lucinda...sleeping her way to the top.* The spark inside of me began to smolder.

"Oh dear," she cried in mock horror. "I've forgotten my manners. Won't you both come in for a spell? It would be just wonderful to catch up with you, baby sister, and I'm just dying to know more about you, Jeff."

As we followed her inside, one word flashed through my mind: *cunt.*

The more things change, the more they stay the same. My sister ushered us in to her nearly spotless apartment, complaining all the while of what a mess it was. Once the door was shut, I was sure that Night Razor would fall upon her, doing whatever he wished while she begged for mercy. I would be forced to watch, compelled to do so if I tried to look away, and powerless to help in the face of his superior strength.

Instead, he complimented her on the décor, accepted a beer - an import, no less - and took a seat on the couch.

What the fuck? Was this part of his game - to completely disarm her before he literally dismembered her? I wouldn't have put it past him. In the nearly two years since I'd come under his watchful eye, I'd come to know that his cruelty had few limits.

That had to be it. I found myself nervously stuck between wanting it over with quickly so she wouldn't suffer and wishing to see it drawn out in the hope that there'd be an opportunity to spare her life. My discomfort didn't go unnoticed.

"You're fidgeting, Lucinda."

"Huh?"

"I said, you're fidgeting." She turned to Night Razor with a sly grin, still shamelessly flirting with him. "Lu was *always* a fidgeter. Used to drive our father crazy. I was always trying to get her to calm down."

Really? That was new. I'd never known her to do anything other than criticize my every choice. Guess I'd missed all of the calming effects her personality radiated.

"How is Dad?" I asked absentmindedly.

"Father is Father, just as he always was. Set in his ways until the day he dies. He certainly didn't approve when I moved out and got a job. Said I needed to find myself a big strong man to settle down with and take care of."

"You look like you're taking care of yourself just fine," Night Razor replied, leaving more than a little room for interpretation in his tone. The fucker was actually flirting back. Despite my lack of a heartbeat, my blood pressure raised a notch.

"But look at you, dear sister," Linda said, turning back to me after holding Night Razor's gaze a second longer than was proper. "You seem to have found yourself a good man. Father would *finally* be so proud. Tell me, Jeff, do you take good care of my little sister?"

"As good as she deserves."

I clenched my fists, barely feeling my claws extend and dig into my palms.

"That's good to hear. Lucinda always did need that extra watchful eye looking out for her. Can I get you another drink, Jeff?"

"Please."

She stood, took Night Razor's empty glass, and walked into the kitchen - not bothering to ask me if I'd like even a first drink. Goddamn, how I'd like to have shattered that glass and rubbed her face in the broken shards.

"Oh, Lucinda," he cooed silently, "your hands."

I looked down and noticed the blood for the first time. Thinking quickly, I wiped my palms on a throw pillow next to me and flipped it over.

"That wasn't very hospitable."

"Can we please get this over with?" I whispered.

"Get what over with?"

"My sister. You dragged me here so I could watch you kill her."

"I did no such thing."

"It's bad enough you have to torture me...I mean, her, with...wait, what do you mean?"

"I'm not going to kill your sister."

"No?" I didn't believe it.

"Why would I? I'm having a perfectly good time."

"But..."

"I will admit, I'm considering recruiting her. She has a certain appeal. However, I haven't made up my mind yet."

He was actually considering making her one of *us*? The fucker actually liked her?! The horror of subjecting my sister to the hell that my existence had become briefly flickered in my head. Outrage quickly replaced the feeling, though, at the thought of spending eternity with the fucking bitch - eons of listening to her strut her superior attitude in my face.

I'd been in her shadow my entire life. She was always prettier, more popular, more to my father's liking. The one thing I had over her, my mind - or so I always thought - had been browbeaten so badly over the years that I'd given up any thought of using it to further my life. Now, here we were: me, little more than an undead whore, and her, the up-and-coming sales manager. She'd become me...or the life I could have, *should have,* lived.

I stepped over to the window and looked out. The view did nothing to quench my rapidly fouling mood. She'd had everything growing up and even now couldn't leave me any scraps. So here was Night Razor, changing his fucking plans like the goddamned asshole he was, and debating offering her the one and only thing I had in my favor: immortality.

No. There was no fucking way that was going to happen.

"Are you okay...*Lucinda?*" Night Razor asked mockingly from his seat.

I bit my tongue. Normally, when he asked a question, he expected an answer. Well, fuck him. If he wanted me to respond, he'd have to compel me.

His voice floated to me from his seat. "Use it."

Use what? What the fuck was he talking about? Goddamnit! I couldn't even think straight. I closed my eyes and massaged my temples with my fingertips, trying to will the anger away. I heard him get up and walk into the kitchen. A few moments later, their voices reached my ears, including my sister's tittering laughter.

I tried to focus, but it was in vain. Whereas normally I would have been able to hear them perfectly, the only sound my ears would focus on was my own ragged breathing, drawing in hitched breaths as I tried to calm myself.

I don't know how long I stood there like that. Could have been seconds or years, for all I knew. Night Razor and Linda continued chatting away in the kitchen. Her continued chuckles at his no doubt asinine comments continued to stab into my consciousness like an ice pick.

An eternity with her...with my cunt of a sister...

Behind me, she reentered the room. "Help your-self, Jeff," she called back.

"Much obliged."

Her footsteps came closer, right up behind me.

"Marvelous view isn't it, Lu? You wouldn't believe what this place costs a month, although I'm happy to say I can afford it."

"What do you mean by that?" I asked through gritted teeth.

"Mean? Just that my position pays quite..."

"No, that I wouldn't believe what this place costs."

"Oh, nothing at all. Your boyfriend was just telling me about your living arrangements...how you share a loft of sorts with some others down in SoHo. Not that there's anything *wrong* with that. I mean, I was never into the Bohemian lifestyle myself, but I'm sure it suits you well in your current *condition*."

"What condition?" I asked, opening my eyes. Facing the window, I wasn't entirely surprised to see that my view of uptown Manhattan had taken on a decisively red hue.

"Well, I suspected as much when you called me back during that time you lived in Vegas, and Jeff tried to dance around the subject a bit, but he did manage to let slip that you do most of your work at night...

I smiled, feeling my fangs elongate. "Oh?"

"And I know you left home in a huff, having barely finished high school. A young, reasonably attractive girl like you...and I imagine the money isn't too bad. I mean, our father would certainly not approve, but I'm not one to judge. They do call it the world's oldest profession for a reason, don't they?" She finished the sentence with a laugh. I was sure she meant it to sound casual, but I could only hear the undertones of pity and scorn in it.

Something in me snapped. The feral nature that I'd felt when I'd taken the lives of Mark and my friends came rushing up to the surface tenfold. This time, though, I let it. It infused every part of me, seeping into the very core of my being.

The old me, the one I'd tried to desperately hold on to, lost her grip. She tumbled into my subconscious, and I was glad to let her go. She was a mouse, whereas the new me was meant to be a lioness. The thing about lionesses, though...they do most of the hunting.

I turned and smiled, knowing what Linda would see. The soulless black orbs that were now my eyes met hers. For a moment there was no response, save for a startled look on her face, then I sensed fear beginning to emanate from her. It lit up her face, made her heart speed up, and flowed from her pores. She backed up a step.

"What's the matter, dear sister?"

"What's...what's wrong with you, Lu?" she replied, trying to sound no more than slightly surprised.

"Nothing at all. I'm just as you said." I took a step closer. "I'm a woman of the night now...only just not quite how you imagined it."

"Please, Lucinda, I never..."

"Oh, and you can stop with that. Your little Lucinda died two years ago. You can call me Sally...at least for this one last moment."

"Jeff!" she screamed, not understanding that he was the last person who would help anyone.

Before she could utter more than his name, I was upon her. Pulling her down to my level, I forced her head to the side, and whispered in her ear. "Let's see if blood truly is thicker than water."

I bit down on her neck, one hand in her hair, yanking her head down further. Her bones creaked, stretched to the limit. I was rewarded for the effort as her blood began to flow down my throat.

There was something different about it from the previous times I'd fed, though. It felt like coming home, although whether it was due to our close relation or my embracing the beast inside of me, I didn't know...or care.

I drank deeply, not wishing to let any of her escape. She'd given me a lifetime of misery, and I meant to repay it to the very last drop.

She attempted to push me away, but in the end, Linda, my older sister, a person who'd lorded her superiority over me at every opportunity, turned out to be a frail thing indeed. Her struggles began to wane. Her heart, which had beaten so frantically when I first attacked, began to slow.

Her heart!

I pulled back for just a moment, long enough for the claws on my right hand to extend. A small voice inside of me, what remained of Lucinda, screamed for me to stop, but I gave it no heed. Her weakness would never dictate my actions ever again.

I slammed my hand into Linda's chest and plowed through her sternum like it was made of tissue paper. A strangled gasp escaped her lips as my fingers closed around her heart.

I pulled it free even as it sputtered its last few beats. Jeff had meant to turn her, but she wouldn't be coming back. I wouldn't allow it.

I tossed the now useless organ over my shoulder and dropped the sack of meat that had been my sister to the floor at my feet.

It was only then that I heard the clapping. Jeff stood in the doorway of the kitchen, his eyes blackened as he applauded me.

Use it.

I realized too late this had been his plan. He had

never meant to kill Linda. It had been me all along. I was meant to sever my ties to the past and become the new me...the life I had struggled so hard to fight.

He walked toward me, continuing to clap as he approached. A part of me wanted to gut him where he stood. The side of me that was now dominant, though, understood and approved. He was a sadistic motherfucker and God help me, but I loved it...wanted more of it.

As he stepped up to me, I grabbed his shirt and tore it open. Before he could say anything else, I pulled him to me and rammed my mouth against his - my teeth tearing furrows across his lips.

I dragged him down, atop of where my sister's body lay, and we began to tear at each other's clothes.

I took him right there as if we were no better than beasts of the night. We were like rabid animals, and I found myself enjoying every sick second of it.

34

As the trio of creatures dragged Mark beneath the roiling water, it wasn't fear that consumed his face, but raw, naked hatred - spite at me and a world that had corrupted him. My decision had been the right one. In the end, he was no better than an animal.

"I'm sorry," I whispered to no one. It was probably more than he deserved.

Another wave of filthy water washed over the catwalk, knocking me to my knees. This time when it subsided, it didn't go down nearly as much. The water level was now two feet above the bottom and rising fast. I grasped the handrail, forced myself back to my unsteady feet, and made the mistake of looking down.

A flash of light shone momentarily, quickly replaced with the glow of malevolent orange eyes - eyes that were rapidly rising again. The creatures meant to have me too.

Make that *us* too. A choking sound reminded me that I wasn't alone. I turned and found Kara doubled over and coughing water out of her lungs. If those things got me, which they surely would if I didn't think of something fast, then she wouldn't be far behind. She was a spoiled little brat of a bitch, but it would be a bad way to die for even her.

What was worse was that nobody, probably not even Christy with her magic - assuming she was still alive - would know what happened. It would be just one of many anonymous deaths to come if these creatures were allowed to surface unchecked from the flooded hell these tunnels had become.

The water bubbled as the monsters neared the surface.

Wait...maybe that was the answer. Hadn't I nearly been swept away by the current? Yet these things were still here because they were made of fucking stone. The goddamn things were basically living anchors.

Me and Kara, on the other hand...

It was all I had left to try. I sloshed back to where she knelt. "Come on!" I said, dragging her up.

"No," she weakly sputtered. "Leave me al..."

She never got a chance to finish her sentence. At that moment, another wave hit us. Without giving it any thought, I grabbed her, digging my claws into her wrist for good measure, and pushed off with my good leg, the rush of water carrying us over the railing.

My body scraped against something sharp. I opened my eyes, and was rewarded with the briefest glimpse of six angry orange eyes fading in the distance of the brackish water as the current swept us away.

Sadly, any victory cry I might have had was cut short - there was no way to scream without inhaling a gallon of sewer water. Being slammed back and forth against the rough rock wall at breakneck speed also wasn't particularly fun.

There was likewise the concern that my reluctant swim mate was going to need air rather soon. She lacked my undead ability to ignore such pesky things.

Unable to halt our forward momentum, I used what little remaining strength I had to kick upward. If we were lucky, we might find a pipe or another catwalk to grab hold of and ride this out until I could think of something better.

Kara desperately clawed at me, no doubt terrified out of her mind. I held fast, though. Just a little more and I'd...*oof!*

My head struck the ceiling and dragged against it. The concrete tore at my scalp and back. Fuck! The tunnel was totally flooded. If there were any pockets of air to be found, we were being pulled along too fast to notice them. Sadly, I didn't have the strength to slow us down. Hell, I was barely able to maintain my own consciousness.

Kara's struggles against me weakened. Fuck! There wasn't any time left. I had to try. I pulled her close to me as we rushed down the flooded sewer tunnel. Wrapping one arm around her waist, I reached out with my claws.

The current slammed us against the wall and I dug in. The pull of the water was monstrously strong, and I dug furrows trying to slow us down, feeling the pain as two of my nails ripped right out.

At last we stopped, although the current threatened to dislodge us at any moment. It was only then that I realized she'd gone completely limp against me. No, goddamnit!

Doing my best while holding on for dear life, I positioned my mouth against hers and realized I had no air left in my lungs to breathe into hers.

It was over.

She was gone, and I wasn't going to be able to hang on much longer in my current condition. I'd be swept along, continually battered until I was either pummeled to paste or those creatures found me.

No! There was one other choice...a way to possibly save us both - and all it meant was throwing my entire reason for doing this out the fucking window.

Her blood.

It would give me the strength to make it through this and would also pave the way for her survival.

I didn't wish it for her. Despite my uncaring demeanor, part of me didn't want her going down the same path. Sadly, there wasn't much choice. History has a way of pissing in your face even as it repeats itself.

There was no time left for further moral debate. I sank my teeth into her neck as the current pulled us free, sending us careening down into the darkness as if we were locked in an eternal embrace.

35

I don't know how long we were under...me feeding, her receiving the gift of damnation. All I knew was that it wasn't a particularly pleasant trip. We were slammed to and fro like we were nothing but flotsam. More than once, Kara's bones snapped from the impact. It wouldn't matter. They'd heal themselves before she awoke. My own wounds begin to mend, even as new ones formed from the battering we took. Such is the way of my...*our*...kind.

The only worry now was those creatures. I doubted they'd give up easily, and I was certain that the number we'd encountered was only the tip of the iceberg. We still needed to find a way out, and for all I knew, having been washed down perhaps miles of tunnels, we may well have been far underground...too far down to...

The rush of water became a deafening roar, and suddenly I surfaced. There wasn't much room over-head - just more dark tunnel. Within moments, however, even that was gone. A brilliant flash of red lightning lit up the sky above me and rain pelted my face as we were ejected from one of Vegas's many flood drains. Concrete rose to either side of us as the flood continued to wash us along.

I'm not sure how far we traveled, but the current finally began to slake. Dragging Kara's inert form, I paddled to the side and managed to claw my way up the embankment, where I collapsed next to her on the rocky ground.

Though there was nothing natural about the storm that continued to rage above us, the rain at least felt good...cleansing. After what we'd been through, I happily accepted it.

I don't know how long we lay there, nor even what time it was. The sky above was dark, save for the oddly colored lightning that signaled the supernatural power within. Power that had, somehow, beckoned those monsters up from the depths.

At long last, though, a sound other than rain or thunder reached my ears - the hum of an engine. A vehicle approached. That was good. We could use a ride. And if the owners asked too many questions, well...what was one more sad story in a city full of them?

There was a squeal of brakes, and then a voice shouted, "Over there!" It sounded familiar. No, it couldn't be...

"Christy?" I asked wearily, trying to sit up.

A person hopped out of the driver's side and quickly approached us. It definitely wasn't her, though. My eyes recognized him a moment before his scent hit my nostrils. It was Barlow's partner, Steve. Fuck!

I had only partially healed, but it would hopefully be enough. I didn't need to be in top form to handle the likes of him...maybe.

Pushing myself to my feet, I extended my fangs and claws - ready to meet him, and vaguely hoping not to be peppered again with gunfire. That would really suck.

To my surprise, though, he skidded to a halt and held up his hands as if in surrender.

"I'm not here to fight."

"Really?" I asked sarcastically. "I suppose you're the rescue party."

"Actually, we are," another voice called out from closer to the car. I hadn't been hearing things earlier. It *was* Christy! What the hell was going on?

She hobbled over, dripping wet and obviously bruised up...but still very much alive.

I smiled despite myself, then quickly reined it in as I remembered Kara lying just a few feet away. How would Christy react to what I'd done?

Her eyes fell to the prone form at my feet. Apparently I was about to find out.

"Kara!" She doubled her pace, passed Steve, and reached us. I took a respectful step back, not quite sure what to say.

Christy dropped to her knees next to the girl and touched her cheek, no doubt noting the cold feel of her skin and the blue pallor of her lips. She pressed her fingers to the side of Kara's neck to feel for the pulse that wouldn't be there.

"Goddamnit," she whispered. She looked up at me and exhaustion reflected in her eyes. Whatever she'd been through since we were separated obviously hadn't been a walk in the park, either. "She's..."

"Going to be okay," I finished. "I made sure of it."

Seeing her questioning eyes, I knelt and turned Kara's head, exposing the puncture marks on the opposite side of her neck.

"What did you..."

"I didn't have a choice. She would have drowned otherwise."

She turned to face me and for a moment, an angry red glow appeared in her eyes. I couldn't blame her. Since becoming involved with vampires, she'd lost a lot: her master and entire coven. Hell, she'd nearly lost her boyfriend not long ago, too. It seemed all we brought her was bad luck. Thus, I didn't take any offense when she said, "Tell me what happened and pray that I believe you."

I relayed everything that occurred: from finding Kara, to Mark nearly gutting me, to our escape from the rock monsters. It was perhaps the longest I'd spoken in years without feeling the need to *elaborate* upon the facts.

When I was finished, Steve again surprised me by backing up parts of my tale, telling of how Mark had sent him and the others on a wild goose chase meant to draw the creatures away.

"Did you realize he was using you as bait?" I asked.

"In my line of work, it pays to not be stupid."

"So what did you do?"

"What do you think? We made a bit of a racket to make it sound good, then I led my group right back toward the entrance as fast as we could."

"That was risky, from more than one point of view."

"Including one that they hadn't been expecting," Christy added.

Turns out she'd been holding a little magic in reserve, just as I'd guessed. Even so, she explained, it'd been close. The rushing water had disoriented her as well as acted like a sort of natural buffer against her magic - something I made a mental note of for future reference. She'd nearly drowned before she got lucky and the spell held.

Somehow, she used the residual magic from the glamour that aided our escape as a sort of homing beacon. Doing so, she was able to *send* herself back to the tunnel entrance - not the safest place in the world to pick, but better than ending up in Davy Jones's sewage-filled locker.

Her timing had apparently been impeccable.

I could only imagine Steve and his group's surprise when she appeared from out of nowhere - dropping to the floor gasping for air, but still with some fight left in her.

Sadly for them...depending on your point of view, of course...the man who'd been closest to her when she appeared also turned out to be the one with a talent for slugging pregnant women in the gut. He and the two people nearest, a human and a vampire, had gotten flash fried before they knew what hit them.

"That really was everything I had. I just didn't let Steve here know it."

"Was a good bluff," he replied, admiration in his voice.

"What did you do?" I asked him.

"Hedged my bets and surrendered. With Marlene dead, I didn't have a quarrel with the witch."

"What about Mark?"

"To tell the truth, I wasn't too fond of him fucking me over."

I smiled. As I'd said, a survivor can always tell another. "What if he'd won?"

"I'd have thought of something," he replied with a similar smile.

"How'd you both find me?"

"When I was holding onto you back in the sewers, I might have plucked a few hairs from your head," Christy admitted. "That makes scrying so much easier." I raised an eyebrow. "In my line of work it also pays to not be stupid," she explained.

I let out a weak laugh. What a team we made. "So what now?"

"Even if I didn't believe you, I'm too tired to do much about it."

"You still could. I don't have a lot of fight left in me."

"Then it's a good thing I do believe you." She reached over and grasped my shoulder. "You could have let Mark kill her. Hell, you could have just left her there. I'm not happy about what you had to do, but I can understand it. Under those circumstances, I'd have done the same thing. Thank you, Sally."

Amazingly enough, nothing particularly pithy came to mind. So I simply replied, "You're welcome." I really needed to get my head examined after this one.

"When is she going to..."

"A couple of hours."

"I can't take her back like this."

"I know."

The threat finally over, Christy's presence seemed to deflate. One moment I wasn't sure if she was going to blast me, and the next she was just a tired expectant mother, barely able to hold herself upright.

She sighed and rubbed her face with her hands. She might have been crying, but I couldn't tell with the rain. "It's too late to stop, isn't it?"

I nodded. "She's too far into the change."

"What am I going to tell Tom and his parents?"

"Tell them the truth. That she's okay."

"But..."

"She will be. I promise you that," I replied, almost shocked to hear the sincerity in my voice. "I have some experience in these things. I'll keep an eye on her, teach her to control herself. Once she's ready, then maybe we can have a happy reunion."

"You'd do that?"

"Village Coven has the openings, and I could use a protégé."

"Pardon my interruption, ma'am," Steve said,

surprising me with his use of the phrase, "but don't you mean Pandora Coven?"

"Why would I?"

"You defeated our coven master...twice, actually...in fair combat. The leadership is rightfully yours."

"But I'm not a member."

"Doesn't matter. There aren't many others left, and those that are I wouldn't trust to lead us out of a paper bag."

"What about you?"

He chuckled. "I'm more of a behind-the-scenes type of guy. I don't like the spotlight...too hazardous."

I stretched, feeling some strength return to my body. The rain was cold, but it felt good against my skin after so much time in the muck. More lightning flashed in the sky, but I wasn't bothered by it. After what I'd been through, it wasn't all that frightening anymore.

I laughed, prepared to tell Steve that regardless of how rudderless his ship was, it still wasn't my problem. The whole world was on the brink, and the only one who stood a chance of stopping it was a frumpy dork who was currently missing. It didn't matter if the threat that the Jahabich represented was something that needed to be...

Wait. *Jahabich*? That's what the monsters below were called.

How the fuck did I know that?

"Sally, are you all right?" Christy asked. "You look funny."

"I'm fine," I replied distractedly. "It's just that I can't..."

I trailed off as the situation unfolded before my eyes. This town was on the verge of collapse. Marlene had done nothing to stem the tide. All she'd been concerned with was sticking her head in the sand and making sure her precious club opened on time. Thanks to her inaction, the creatures had gotten their current foothold.

I thought of all the girls the club employed, the empty shelter we'd found underground, the countless others who were helpless in the face of everyday life in this city - much less the growing darkness beneath it. I was once one of them. Fate had failed me, but now I had a chance to repay it and make good.

I couldn't leave.

"Sally?" Steve and Christy exchanged glances in the downpour, but I paid them no mind.

You won't remember this part until you need to.

My eyes momentarily lost focus as the force of the memory...of the compulsion...came pouring into my consciousness.

Goddamnit...James!

"There, that should do it. You'll be able to resist Marlene's orders for a time. Be warned, though - a remote compulsion over the phone isn't as strong. I'd suggest you make haste."

"Thank you..."

"Don't thank me. I'm most likely sending you to your death, regardless." Something about the tone of his voice, though, told me he didn't believe that. It was that wry humor of his, almost undetectable at times, but we'd done this dance before.

"You wouldn't be doing this if you thought I was walking into my death."

"Wouldn't I?"

"No."

"Well then, let's just say I have faith in your skills. You are a survivor, my dear. I've known that about you since the day we met."

"So you're condoning revenge."

"Not in the least."

"Then why?"

He sighed and the base of my skull tingled a moment before I heard his voice.

"*YOU WON'T REMEMBER THIS PART UNTIL YOU NEED TO!! BUT WHEN YOU DO, KNOW THAT I DO THIS BECAUSE I BELIEVE IN YOU!!*"

My eyes lost focus on the room around me. I couldn't have put down the phone, spoken, or done much of anything had I tried. I'd nearly forgotten just how powerful he was.

"Marlene is a liability," James explained. "She refuses to acknowledge the threat to her city, and at the same time is fiercely resistant to any and all who try to stake a claim of authority within her realm. I do not wish her removal, but it has become a necessity. She must be replaced, but it must be done delicately. It can't be someone with the power to simply waltz in and destroy her. That would anger the neighboring covens and force the prefect of the West Coast to investigate. At the same time, it must be done by someone with the competence to hold the line."

He went on, telling me of the Jahabich, an ancient threat that had been driven below the earth ages ago. They were neither aligned with us nor our enemies, the Feet. They were beings of pure chaos - destroying for nothing more than their own amusement. Though Las Vegas was not strategically important in our war, if allowed to gain a foothold, these creatures would spread like a cancer from city to city...our domains, thus undermining us at a time when we needed it least.

The memory slammed into me, tearing through the door in which it had been locked. I had left New York thinking it was possible this was a one-way trip.

Now it seemed that it had been pre-ordained from the very start.

Was that all I was to him, just another puppet to be used? Another pawn in this war? I opened my mouth to scream out my frustration. Was there nobody in the world who wasn't trying to use me for their own purpose?

The cry wouldn't come, though. My thoughts scattered again...the memories weren't quite finished.

James continued, telling me of the need for someone to take over and fight back. The City of Sin had a backbone of the supernatural. There were resources that could be marshaled against the threat, but diluted - leaderless - they would fall.

"Know that I serve the greater good and am willing to do things, dark things, to preserve it," he said. "I know under normal circumstances you would never even consider accepting this great responsibility. Dr. Death's return weighs heavily on you. Despite whatever you might say to the contrary, I am well aware of it. But the truth is, we simply don't know when or if he will be back."

I waited silently for it...for the compulsion to come that would steal my choice away from me and make me just another cog in the wheels of fate.

But it never came.

"Even knowing that, though, I cannot bring myself to do it. You've been a friend, Sally, a confidant. I see some of myself in you...and not in the way Dr. Death might mention."

Despite the initial compulsion, a smirk rose to my face. Yeah, if Bill ever knew of our past, he'd never shut the fuck up about it.

"Despite everything, every dark decision you've ever made or will make going forward, I believe you are stepping toward the light again. I told you once that the day might come when you'd be reminded of your humanity. I sense that time has come to pass. The old you has woken from her slumber and joined hands with the new. I won't compel you, but I'm hiding this memory for now because I think it might taint your decision...raise your defense mechanisms, so to speak."

James was many things to me: friend, former lover, mentor...and with his next words, I realized a father figure, too - one I'd been sorely lacking my entire life.

"The choice is yours to make, but I believe you will make the right one."

I'd been manipulated by so many people in my life: Colin, Marlene, Jeff, Mark. The list went on and on, but it seemed that perhaps it was finally over.

I looked Christy in the eye and smiled to let her know it was all right, *I* was all right. There was a lot of work to be done, but despite everything, I felt up to the challenge.

It was time to finally take ownership of my life.

EPILOGUE

I cupped my hand over the receiver. "Quit whining, Kara, and get back to work." She stuck her tongue out at me - real mature - and stormed out.

"I take it your newest recruit is a little rough around the edges."

"You heard that, James?"

"I wasn't trying to, of course."

"Sure you weren't. My God, what a little bitch she can be. Still, she is showing promise. Only a month in and she's proven herself capable. Once you dig past the self-absorbed seventeen-year-old exterior, there's actually a functional brain there. She's proven to have a knack for sniffing out particularly adept recruits."

"No doubt handy during these dark times."

"Don't get me wrong, she still has a long way to go." Her only partially mature hormones, combined with the hunger, were proving difficult for her to overcome. She'd had a few episodes...ones that I'd neglected to fill Christy in on during her daily phone calls to check on us.

"Of course. But good things with time. She has an excellent teacher."

"Flattery will get you everywhere."

"I'm glad to hear it. How goes the defense?"

"We're getting there. I've been making good on Marlene's contacts with the mages in town. They're still going to maintain their neutrality if any shit breaks out with the Feet, but against those fucking rock things, they're willing to help. Good thing, too; the goddamn things are tough, nearly impervious to blunt force trauma. Add enough heat, though, and they become statues. It's a good partnership. We provide the muscle, and they bring the firepower. These things are smart, though. They're not going to go down easily."

"Well then it's a good thing they're up against a force they have no chance of outwitting."

"You knew I'd choose to stay," I said, changing topics.

"I knew no such thing."

"Bullshit."

"Seriously. I gave it a fifty-fifty chance at best."

"Thanks for not compelling me."

"The right choice can't be compelled. It can only be freely chosen."

For the hundredth time since Bill had disappeared, I asked James if he'd heard anything as we wrapped up our call, and for the equal amount of times, he told me no. Had this crap all gone down immediately after the ordeal with the Icon, James would have been sorely disappointed in my final decision. Now, though...

The truth was, four months in, the sting was starting to wear off a bit. I still held out hope, but my refusal to just stand idly by and wait tempered it.

That didn't mean there weren't still some worries back east. With me out here, I'd been forced to cede coven leadership in New York. It's rare to change management of a coven without bloodshed. I sure as hell couldn't recall another example of it ever happening. Thankfully, as even Colin - the little shit - had to grudgingly admit when I called to inquire, there was a seldom used rule on the books granting right to choose a successor to the outgoing master.

Starlight was now in charge. She wasn't the most senior in the coven, and I had little doubt those politics would come into play. Fortunately, my final orders as leader to Monkhbat had included that he watch out for such shenanigans and deal with them accordingly.

That still left Firebird. She'd thoroughly fucked me over and no doubt was thinking she'd gotten away with it. Let her. She could go about her nights, offering her wares up to whomever she pleased. Her main sources of favor, Jeff and Marlene, were gone. She was just an undead whore now - toothless in a sense of the word. Besides, much like the vulture, I'm a patient bird. She'd get hers, and when that happened, I planned on being there. At the very least, it gave me something to look forward to.

I stood up from my desk and stretched. The club would be opening soon. Dusk was approaching, and thankfully there were clear skies ahead. Those fucking monsters tended to only come out right before and during a storm. Not sure why, but I hadn't had much time to research it yet. I'd eventually figure it out and when I did, I'd take that knowledge and ram it down their throats.

Steve and his hunting party would be returning soon, hopefully with a few more kills. The Jahabich were tough, but they tended to be solitary; never in groups of more than three or so. By systematically searching for them rather than waiting for the fuckers to come to us, we maintained the status quo.

Interestingly enough, life had begun to return to the tunnels. The downtrodden were starting to set up shop close to the club's underground entrance. They didn't ask questions, but seemed to know we were doing what we could.

The irony of it all made me laugh. Humans - our prey - were now flocking to us for protection. What had the world come to?

I walked to the one-way mirror of Marlene's former office, now my executive suite, and surveyed the club below. Fate had quite the sense of irony putting me in charge here. Even so, despite the oddness of the situation, it felt somehow natural.

James had been more right than I cared to admit. Watching the bartenders and DJ set up below, I smiled. Hopefully theirs, as well as the girls who were even now prepping for the night ahead, were lives that would be allowed to continue. While some had been, or would be, recruited to our side, many more would be able to go about their days ignorant that anything was amiss.

For a while, anyway.

I wasn't about to fool myself. There was still the upcoming war. The very Earth would potentially be torn asunder as our forces clashed with those of our enemies. The end times were very much nigh.

Still, until such time as that happened, my place was here. I would hold the line no matter what. I would...

My cell phone rang, interrupting my thoughts. Figuring that perhaps it was Christy, calling for the umpteenth time to check on Kara, I lifted it and saw an unfamiliar number. That was odd. It wasn't a Boston area code, either.

I clicked to answer it and brought it to my ear, hoping it wasn't a telemarketer. If so, I'd track their ass down and...

"Sally? Is that you?"

My mouth froze halfway open at the sound of his voice.

"Jesus Christ, where the *fuck* are you? You have no idea the shit I've been through."

No, not now!

There came a crash on the other end of the call, like a wrecking ball had just plowed through a wall.

"I've...sorta...fucked up, just a little bit. I kinda need your help...oh shit!"

More commotion exploded out of the receiver. It sounded like World War Three had broken out.

I finally found my voice. "Bill?"

But the line was already dead. What the fuck had just happened? Had I imagined it? Was it some sort of hallucination brought on by post-traumatic stress? Was maybe someone messing with me right when I'd found my peace with the world?

I looked down at the handset. At the very least, I'd definitely received a call. I dialed the number back and held it to my ear. It rang...three...five...times before switching over to a generic answering message.

For a long time after, I stood and watched the club come to life below me, but didn't really see it.

It isn't fair!

This was home now...where it had all started for me. It was a chance to right my wrongs and make sure history didn't repeat itself for anyone else. James had entrusted it to me. He sent me here, knowing I'd make the right choice. He'd believed in me.

Could I throw that all to the wayside for one life-less fucking dork with a penchant for screwing up every single thing he fucking touched? Hell, I couldn't even be sure it had really been him.

It had to have been a mistake...or a trick...or maybe I'd somehow developed brain damage at some point in the...

Goddamnit!

I let out a long sigh. Was there really any choice?

Actually, I mused, there was. For perhaps the first time in my life, I was in charge of my own fate.

James had said he'd trusted me to make the right decision, but I realized now he'd been very coy as to what that choice was. Perhaps it was still waiting to be made.

Maybe I was the only one who could truly decide what that was.

That crafty son of a bitch!

Looking at the glass that separated me from the club below, I momentarily caught a glimpse of my reflection. I wasn't surprised in the least to see a big smile plastered on my face.

I turned back toward my desk. There was a lot of work to be done to keep this city...this world...from going straight to Hell. I, for one, intended to play my part, but in my own way. My days as a pawn were over. The right choice would be whatever I deemed it.

I grinned and considered my next course of action. Whatever I chose, I'd make sure as shit that it counted.

Fate could be a bitch, but it had nothing on me.

THE END

Sally Sunset will return in:
Goddamned Freaky Monsters
(The Tome of Bill - 5)

BONUS CHAPTER
GODDAMNED FREAKY MONSTERS

The Tome of Bill Part 5

ARISE, FREEWILL!!

Ugh. There are few things that can fuck up a good night's sleep quite like the goddamned alarm clock going off.

I stretched and sat up, feeling as if I'd slept for weeks. A yawn escaped my lips and I blinked several times as my body continued *booting up*. Once my head was clear, I put my glasses on - snapping things into focus.

Before it could go off again, I smacked the button on the clock - giving it a good whack to drive the point home. Jeez, what a stupid alarm. Who the hell would program something like that into a clock, anyway? It had to have been my roommates fucking with me...*again*. The dickheads seemed to have a hard-on for doing so.

Oh well, it was probably time to get my ass

moving. It's not like the work day was going to start without me.

I hopped right into my morning routine, pausing only momentarily as I tried to think of what was on the docket for the day. Surely there was some fire to be put out - a project due that was probably giving Jim, my manager at Hopskotchgames.com, a near aneurysm. It was the same thing week after week. Sure, it could get annoying, but there was a certain comfort in the routine of it all.

The only problem was that I had no idea which project needed tending to. Was it *Farm Fury*? No, we launched that already. Maybe *Birds of War*? Could be *Doctor Dexter's Daring Dash* - that one was coming soon...I think.

Odd. Usually, I was pretty spot on for my schedule, but for the life of me, I had no clue what I was supposed to be working on. Hell, come to think of it, I had no idea what *day* it even was. It could have been the freaking weekend for all I knew.

But then, why the alarm clock? Oh well. It would probably sort itself out as the morning progressed.

Trying to ignore the concern that nagged at me, I grabbed my clothes and headed toward the bathroom. Hopefully, it would be unoccupied and there would still be some hot water left. Surely a shower would help clear my head.

Just as I sat on the couch, a bowl of Cap'n Crunch in hand, a sense of déjà vu hit me. That was stupid. I mean, *of course* I'd done this before. I lived in this place, for Christ's sake. I'd probably eaten hundreds of bowls of tooth-rotting cereal sitting right in this spot.

I shook it off as part of the general paranoia that had become a part of my existence ever since dying and rising from the proverbial grave as a vampire. The supernatural world was a fucked-up place, and it seemed that I couldn't take a dump without some entity deciding that I needed to be vaporized. Such things tended to mess with one's outlook on life after a while.

Well, fuck that shit. The worries of the underworld could wait until after I'd had my breakfast.

I flipped on the TV, enjoying the rare moment of normalcy. Well, that wasn't entirely true. Hell, a disturbing amount of my life remained mundane. There was my job, for starters - believe me, becoming one of the undead hadn't been an instant lottery ticket to riches. There were also my roommates...

Speaking of which, where the hell were they?

I guess it made sense that Tom had either left early for his job in Manhattan or maybe slept over at his girlfriend's place, but Ed worked from home like me. There wasn't anything requiring him to be in the office today, at least that I could remember, and last night was...

I paused, a spoonful of cereal halfway to my mouth. Last night was what? That was a blank too. It couldn't have been too memorable. I mean, heck, the apartment wasn't even close to being trashed. At the very least, I should've had some remembrance of what show I'd watched or video game I'd played, but there was nothing.

Don't get me wrong. I didn't seem to be suffering from amnesia or any bullshit like that. The important stuff was all there: who I was, my job, where I lived - that kind of shit. It was just the recent past that eluded me for some reason.

I had to admit - it was starting to get odd.

Maybe we had all gone...

Come to think of it, when was the last time I had even *seen* my roommates?

No, that was stupid. We were the best of friends. We hung out all the time...even when the forces of evil were trying to collectively ass-fuck us.

Weird. Maybe I drank a few bottles of overly skunked beer last night and it was screwing with my brain. That didn't sound so farfetched. If so, my vampire metabolism would take care of it as the day went on, hopefully allowing the fog to lift from my head.

Yeah, I'd let things sort themselves out. There was probably no point in worrying.

I bit down with a satisfying crunch, then began scanning through the channels, hoping to find something worth watching.

Not wanting to burden my soul with *Good Morning America* or similar insipid morning shit, I quickly skipped to the cable channels - finally stopping on what looked to be some sort of action flick.

There was a battle taking place on a rooftop. Multi-colored lightning flashed in the background as the combatants recklessly tore into each other - gotta love low-budget sci-fi. Yeah, this had promise.

A glowing blonde angel was trashing the bad guys in the middle of it all. Damn, she was hot. Hopefully, this flick had some nudity in it. That wouldn't exactly be a horrible way to start the day.

Another character, this one decked out in a SpongeBob backpack of all things, hopped onto the screen and began similarly kicking ass. She looked to be of roughly schoolgirl age. Maybe this was a Japanese fetish flick. Talk about a country that was seriously fucked in the head when it came to entertainment.

I was about to change the channel and see what else was playing when my hand paused on the remote. The walking Nickelodeon advertisement was tackled from the side and dragged screaming off the edge. It should have been hilarious. I mean, seriously, I've never seen a Wilhelm scream scene that didn't crack me up. Something about this bothered me, though.

That déjà vu feeling hit me again like a brick to the forehead.

No idea why, but the whole thing felt oddly familiar, and not in a good way. Sadness filled me at the poor little character's demise. As the rest of the scene unfolded before me, I actually had to reach up and wipe a few tears from my eyes.

I quickly glanced around, making sure neither of my roommates was present to see my sensitive side coming out to play. I'd never hear the end of that.

After a few moments - satisfied that I was still alone - I turned back to see how things played out.

The battle seemed to be over. The angel stood there, victorious. She was still wearing too much clothing for my personal gratification, but nevertheless, I was tempted to stand up and cheer for her. Then I noticed one of the bad guys was still alive and approaching from her blind side.

I actually shouted, "No!" at the screen as he pulled out a ridiculously large gun and pointed it at the blonde Xena's head. A bullet to her face ended the showdown.

I stared transfixed, wondering how the director could allow such a downer of an ending. Asshole should've been fired. Things weren't quite over yet, though. Apparently in need of a fucked-up finale to finish things off with, a bad CGI monster - some kind of Hulk rip-off - jumped into frame from out of nowhere and began tearing shit up.

Okay, this was getting a little too *out there,* even for me - which was strange in and of itself. Normally, I enjoyed fucked-up foreign movies, but this one had left a bad taste in my mouth for some reason.

I clicked off the television and placed my bowl down, my appetite gone too.

Standing up, I turned my thoughts toward work. Heck, after watching that shit, I was actually looking forward to it. Maybe a few hours of coding would slap me out of my funk. I still had no idea exactly what I was supposed to be programming, but maybe that didn't matter. Hell, worst-case scenario was I would wing it - maybe take a stab at creating something from scratch. It's not like Jim would say no to some extra...

A knock at the door interrupted my train of thought.

I waited for a moment, making sure I hadn't imagined it, but then it came again. Hmm, kind of early for visitors.

Not thinking too much of it, I stood up and walked over - assuming one of my wayward room-mates had locked himself out again. In the back of my head, thoughts of wizards, vampire assassins, and angry Sasquatches played out, but I dismissed them all. Most of those, especially that last group, probably wouldn't have bothered knocking. Besides, I lived in the middle of Brooklyn - not exactly prime Bigfoot country.

Chuckling at my own paranoia, I reached for the knob. As the door opened, though, the sound instantly died in my throat. For a moment, I could do nothing but gape in stunned silence.

The person who stood there was quite familiar to me. I'd have known him anywhere, even with the black eyes and razor sharp fangs.

How could I not? It was me.

Yeah, my day had just gotten a wee bit stranger.

Goddamned Freaky Monsters
Available now!

ABOUT THE AUTHOR

Rick Gualtieri lives alone in central New Jersey with only his wife, three kids, and countless pets to both keep him company and constantly plot against him. When he's not busy monkey-clicking words, he can typically be found jealously guarding his collection of vintage Transformers from all who would seek to defile them.

Defilers beware!

THE TOME OF BILL UNIVERSE

THE TOME OF BILL
Bill the Vampire
Scary Dead Things
The Mourning Woods
Holier Than Thou
Sunset Strip
Goddamned Freaky Monsters
Half A Prayer
The Wicked Dead
Shining Fury
The Last Coven

BILL OF THE DEAD